LISA SUZANNE

LONG GAME
VEGAS ACES BOOK TWO
© 2021 Lisa Suzanne

All rights reserved. In accordance with the US Copyright Act of 1976, the scanning, uploading, and sharing of any part of this book without the permission of the publisher or author constitute unlawful piracy and theft of the author's intellectual property. No part of this book may be reproduced or transmitted in any form or by any means, electronic or mechanical, including photocopying, recording, or by any information storage and retrieval system without the written permission of the author, except where permitted by law and except for excerpts used in reviews. If you would like to use any words from this book other than for review purposes, prior written permission must be obtained from the publisher.

Published in the United States of America by Books by LS, LLC.

ISBN: 9798708587848

This book is a work of fiction. Any similarities to real people, living or dead, is purely coincidental. All characters and events in this work are figments of the author's imagination.

Cover Designed by Najla Qamber Designs
Content Editing by It's Your Story Content Editing
Proofreading by Proofreading by Katie

BOOKS BY LISA SUZANNE

A LITTLE LIKE DESTINY SERIES
A Little Like Destiny (Book One)
Only Ever You (Book Two)
Clean Break (Book Three)

MY FAVORITE BAND STANDALONES
Take My Heart
The Benefits of Bad Decisions
Waking Up Married
Driving Me Crazy
It's Only Temporary
The Replacement War

Visit Lisa on Amazon for more titles

DEDICATION

To the 3Ms who are part of my Long Game.

CHAPTER 1

"Fuck." He sighs, and *dammit* I wish I could read him better. Is he muttering curses because of the article? Because he believes it? Because of how it's going to affect his image?

And then it's like something flips. He blinks as he stares off into space for a second. "Oh, shit."

"What?"

He grabs the towel from around his neck and hangs it over the side of the treadmill. "We had a bonus night." He avoids eye contact as he stares down at his towel as realization seems to crash into him. "Fuck."

"A bonus night?" I ask, my brows furrowing.

He nods and rubs the back of his neck. "Yeah. Two months ago maybe? It was after we broke up." He tries to think back as he turns and stares out into his yard. "I was out with a group of buddies, and we drank way too much, and she showed up at my place. I was drunk and we...well, you know."

"Banged?" I fill in the blank, and he's the one looking all awkward now.

He clears his throat. "Yeah."

I wave my phone around. "You think what's in the article is true?"

He nods as he grips his hair with both hands, the first real emotion he's shown during this conversation apart from some cursing. "She's manipulative, but she wouldn't lie about something like this to the media." His hair is sticking up as he punches one fist into the palm of his other hand. "Dammit. I should've known she was going to find some way to trap me. And to run to Savannah..." He shakes his head. "That's just bullshit."

"This doesn't mean you're trapped, Luke. Plenty of parents raise kids just fine without being married."

"Yeah, but you don't know Michelle. She's the kind of person who would get pregnant on purpose to find a way to keep me in her life." He grips the railing of the treadmill, and then he sits on the belt. He hangs his head as anger melts into wistfulness. "Jesus. I'm going to be a father. This is not at all how I expected today to go."

I kneel on the ground across from him so we're eye level. "She can manipulate all she wants, Luke, but you don't have to be with her even if you're having a baby with her. You can be *there* for her. You can *support* her. But you don't have to be her boyfriend or her husband."

He glances up at me, and he has this torn look in his eyes. He wants to do what's right, but he also wants to live his own life. He wants to be happy. He doesn't want to be trapped by someone he doesn't see in his life forever...even if she *will* be in his life in some capacity if she really is carrying his baby.

And I don't believe for a second that it's really his. He can believe her all he wants, but I don't have to.

"All right, publicist," he says. He glances up at me, and when our eyes connect, even amid this scandal that I'm going to have to sort for him, I feel the heat between the two of us. "Prove your worth."

My eyes widen, and I nod. "I've got this."

"I'll get you a ring today," he says. "A bigger one than the one she wanted."

I laugh at the sheer pettiness in his tone, but I'm not sure I quite get what's happening. "So just like that...we're engaged?"

He presses his lips together. "Looks like it."

"But it's fake," I clarify.

He stares at me a long beat as if he's contemplating his next move, and then he shrugs before he speaks the words that knock my knees out from under me. "It doesn't have to be...not if we actually get married."

My jaw drops and my eyes widen as I stare at him in stunned silence. When I finally manage to form words, I stammer. "Uh...what?"

He chuckles.

"Are you suggesting we really get *married*?" I ask.

"With that reaction, I'll slowly back away and say *no*, that wasn't what I was suggesting. It was just a thought." He lifts a shoulder.

My brows dip as I think about it. "I thought you didn't want to get married ever again."

"I don't. But our engagement's public now. It's in black and white," he says nodding to the headline on my phone. "Michelle plays games. I've never played back, but you know what? I thought a lot about what you said yesterday, and I think you're right."

"What *I* said?" I ask. My cheeks are all hot just from having this conversation. I'm pretty sure I'm sweating, and I'm still in that damn flimsy tank top and shorts. "What did I say?"

"That what she does isn't fair." He pauses, and then he shakes his head. "You're right. It isn't. If I want things to change with Michelle, then I have to make them change. I need her to see I'm committed to somebody else, that this trick she's trying to pull won't work. If she's carrying my kid, I'll be the best dad I can be. But I can't be *with* her. This engagement plan is crazy enough to work...if you're still on board with it."

"I'm still on board with the *engagement*," I say.

I may need a minute on the *actual marriage* topic of conversation. I'm pretty sure he was just kidding, anyway. Wasn't he?

My eyes fall to his abs.

Is it really such a crazy idea?

That's clearly the lust talking, but still...

The thought of his hips slamming against my backside as I clawed at the floor-to-ceiling windows in a hotel room on the Las Vegas Strip flashes through my mind.

Did it just get a little hotter out here?

I blow out a breath.

I don't know about the marriage thing, but as far as a fake engagement is concerned, I have nothing to lose here. I'll help him however I can.

Not because he's hot (though he is), and not because I have a huge crush on him (though I do), but because he's letting me stay here and he's giving me a job and he's my brother's best friend. It's really not a big deal to pretend to be engaged to the hottest guy I've ever laid eyes on.

"Get back on that treadmill," I say. I need to change the subject. "We're about to set some thirst traps on your Instagram."

"Thirst traps?" he asks as he gets back on the treadmill as requested.

"Oh, my sweet husband to be, you have so much to learn. Start running."

"Right now? Don't we need to deal with this pregnancy thing first? Shouldn't I call Michelle or something?" he asks.

"That's exactly what she wants, isn't it? I'll handle the media angle, but we need a second to think it through. Let's take a deep breath and draft a plan before you run to the phone. And in the meantime, I'll take some photos so we can get your Insta-campaign moving."

His brows furrow and God he's adorable, but then he does what I ask. I relish my job as his amateur photographer, snapping different angles of him as he runs on the treadmill. I blush even harder as I think how I'm building quite the spank bank.

And that's when I remember I literally rolled out of bed to come down here. My hair is a mess, I have morning breath, I'm not wearing any make-up, and I'm donning that awful tank top with a pair of short, barely-there shorts.

As he looks over in my direction, though, and his eyes flick down the length of my body...it doesn't appear that he cares that I just rolled out of bed.

In fact, he almost seems to like it.

The heat in his eyes makes me feel that way, anyway.

I chalk that look in his eyes up to him sweating on his treadmill. I take a few more photos, let him know I'm heading inside, and I go up to my bedroom to shower.

After I scroll through all the images I just took, of course.

Once I'm dressed and my teeth are brushed, I find Luke in the kitchen pouring Lucky Charms cereal into a bowl. "Want some?" he asks.

I shake my head and move toward the massive refrigerator to check out Debbie's breakfast options.

"There's a fresh pot of coffee," he says.

"Do you have any flavored coffee cream?" I ask from the depths of the fridge.

He nods. "Top shelf on the left."

Once I have my coffee, I carefully slide onto the stool and pull up the photos I took of Luke on my phone. I pick out one of my favorites, do a little light editing, and whip up a caption that mentions how he loves his job and works hard to keep his body field ready even in the offseason.

"Ready for your first post to Instagram?" I ask him.

He glances over at me, and I snap a picture of him pouring milk into his cereal bowl. It's such a normal, everyday thing for a guy to be doing in his kitchen, but it shows him in an element very few people have ever seen him in. He looks warily at me for a beat then grabs a spoon and steps toward me. "Show me what you've got."

I slide my phone over to him, and he looks at the picture and then up at me.

I grin. "That, my friend, is what we in the business call a *thirst trap*."

"Yeah, you said that before and I still don't know what it means."

"It's when you post a hot pic with the intention of getting attention," I explain. "The more likes and comments you get on a photo, the more Instagram will see that you're a worthwhile user, and the more they'll show your account to other people."

"And that picture of me, a sweaty mess from running all morning...that's a thirst trap?" He looks at me with disbelief, and I giggle.

"You have no idea how hot you are, do you?" I ask.

He raises his brows. "I worked up a pretty good sweat, so yeah, I have some concept of how hot I was."

I roll my eyes. "You know what I meant."

He laughs. "That doesn't make it any less weird that you're telling me how hot I am like it's no big deal before I've even had my cereal. It's a big deal, Ellie."

"Why?" I challenge. "You already told me I'm off-limits. I work for you now, and my goal is to show the world how hot you are, how kind you are, and, above all, how essential you are to the Aces. It all starts with thirst trap number one. So do I have your approval?"

"God, you really like making me step out of my comfort zone." He sighs heavily, and then he shrugs. "Go ahead. Do what I'm paying you to do, and if I live to regret it, well, then that's on me."

"You won't live to regret it. Just trust me." I click the post button and cross my fingers that I'm doing all the right things to help him and that neither of us will live to regret my words.

CHAPTER 2

Prove your worth.

Despite all the other words he said to me—like the fact that he's going to get me a (huge-ass) ring so we can really be pretend-engaged and maybe really get married even though I still think he was just kidding about that—those three are the ones that keep playing on repeat.

I need to figure out how to spin this news.

It's now my job to make him look like the good guy for being engaged to one woman when he knocked someone else up.

I sigh as I stare at the blinking cursor on a very blank screen.

I've got my work cut out for me.

No matter what way I spin this, he comes out looking like a horny douchebag.

Unless it isn't really his baby.

I need to find out how far along she is. I need some sort of concrete evidence that it might be his. "Luke?" I yell across the house.

"Yeah?" he yells back. I think he's in his office, and he walks into the kitchen a few seconds later. "What's going on?"

"When was your bonus night?"

His brows push together, and then he squints like he's trying to think back and I see the moment it clicks almost like a lightbulb going off above his head. He pulls his phone out of his pocket, opens an app, and counts. "Seven weeks ago this past Saturday. We went out for Bryant's birthday."

"Who's Bryant?"

He gives me a you-can't-be-serious kind of look, but he answers anyway. "Jaxon Bryant? Star running back of the Aces?" He says them like questions, and I just shrug because I still don't know who he is.

He shakes his head and laughs. "I've never met anyone who didn't know a thing about the game, let alone a blood relative of a player."

I hold up both hands. "Sorry! Josh has only been playing here a year. Ask me about a player on the Bears and maybe I'd know." That's a lie. I wouldn't know.

"Was that your only question?" he asks. "I'm going through some paperwork from my agent."

"When did you break up?" I ask.

"I don't know. A few months ago?"

"Not good enough. I'm trying to figure out your spin here, and you're not giving me much to work with. So unless you want to come off looking like a d-bag who can't keep it in his pants, I need a date."

He stares at me for a beat in a bit of shock, and then he raises a brow and shoots me a sly smile. "I like when you get all authoritative over me even if what you just said was really kind of mean."

I know I'm blushing, but I force myself not to react to his words. Instead, I raise my brows in a silent way of asking what his answer is.

He blows out a breath, and then he looks at his phone again. I peek over and see him scrolling through his calendar, and I bet if I asked Michelle when they broke up, she'd have a date and time down to the minute.

"It was January, right after we lost the playoffs. She thought she was being cute when she called me a loser, and that was it. I was done."

"What a bitch," I say. "And you still gave her a bonus night?"

"I was so fucked up I don't even remember it," he says. He slides his phone back into his pocket. "She was there when I woke up in the morning. We were both naked. I put two and two together."

"You were wasted, banged a woman you can't stand, don't remember it, and she shows up claiming she's carrying your baby a convenient seven weeks later?" I ask. It's not adding up, and I don't trust Michelle. But I have to find a way to make Luke look like a good guy without tearing down a pregnant Michelle to the press. Public sympathy will be on the pregnant lady's side regardless of how I spin it.

"Yeah, that about sums it up," he says. "What are you suggesting?"

"Maybe a paternity test? I don't know how these things work, but I can research it for you."

He clears his throat. "I might have some experience there."

I raise a brow, and he sighs.

"Total transparency, after my divorce, I made some really dumb decisions."

I have some questions about all that, but I log them and push them to the back of my brain because I have a problem to solve here.

"Okay, before I send out your statement, you need to talk to her," I say. "Call her right now. Demand proof that she's pregnant and that it's really yours."

He stares at me for a beat, and then he slides onto the stool next to me. "I'll demand evidence she's really knocked up, but I can't just call her and demand a paternity test."

"Why not?"

"It's complicated." He doesn't wait for me to reply to that. Instead, he dials her number and puts her on speaker so I can listen in.

"Luke, my darling," she answers. "I've been waiting for your call."

He rolls his eyes, and I stifle a giggle. "I need proof you're really pregnant."

"I had my first doctor's appointment two days ago," she says. "I'm seven weeks along. They put my date of conception on April fifth, and that's the night we slept together. I came by to tell you about the baby but you didn't seem interested in conversation."

"So you ran to Savannah?" he sneers.

"I had to do something to get your attention, my dear."

I want to reach into the phone and rip her head off.

"I want proof you're really pregnant," Luke says again.

"I'll screenshot the paperwork from my doctor over when we hang up. Maybe me smiling with my little stick of pee. Will that be good enough for you?"

"It'll do for now, but I want proof from your doctor."

"Yes, sir. God, I miss when you used to get all dominating on me." Her voice comes out in a moan, and I guess this is her way of coming onto him.

I raise a brow at him. Dominating? Interesting.

My thighs clench at the thought of him demanding things from me while we're both naked. Thoughts of sex up against a window in a hotel room crash into me.

Again.

I blow out a breath. That night really turned all this into a complicated mess. If I was just living with my brother's best friend and I had a crush on him, that would be one thing.

But I can remember his body against mine. I remember him sliding in and out of me. I remember kissing him.

Butterflies batter around in my stomach.

This isn't good.

"Well I'm marrying another woman, so you'll just have to go on missing it." He ends the call, and I raise my hand up for a high five.

He twists his lips as he slaps my hand with his, like he doesn't really want to celebrate the call.

"Good work, my darling Luke," I say.

He narrows his eyes at me. "You better watch it. I haven't forgotten that your brother calls you Ellie Belly."

My cheeks burn and I change the subject. "What's our story?"

He looks confused, so I clarify.

"What will we tell people when they ask how we met?"

"We met through Josh," he says as he starts sorting our pretend meet cute. "Maybe you were out here for a weekend when he first moved here and we met and kept in touch. You decided to move here more recently because I proposed."

I shake my head. "My ex, Todd, the one who I got fired for banging in the office…" I trail off when he winces.

Why did he wince?

Is it because he feels some sympathy over me getting fired?

Or is it because he doesn't want to think of me having sex with somebody else?

Add the wince to the list of things I'll overanalyze tonight when I'm trying to fall asleep.

"Yeah?" he says with a tone that urges me to continue.

"I feel like he's pretty pissed at me over what happened and I wouldn't put it past him to blow that story up," I say, trying to think through all the angles. "We need something more airtight."

"Okay, then we met through Josh about a year ago. Does that part work?" he asks. I nod, and he continues. "We kept in touch. We got to know each other over the distance. We both had feelings but the timing never worked out so we were just good friends. And then you came out here for the wedding, we were both finally single at the same time, and within days, we knew it was right and we got engaged."

I lift a shoulder. "It could work. Some people won't believe in the insta-love, though."

"Insta-love?" His brows crunch together.

"Like we instantly fell in love."

"We didn't," he says, shaking his head. "We'll say we met a year ago. We kept in touch. We both fell in love over the course of time, and when we finally had the chance to be together, we grabbed it. That's not instant love."

"Insta-love," I correct, and he laughs and holds up both hands.

"Okay, okay. Whatever. Does that story work for you?"

I nod slowly, my lips pressed together. "I think it could work."

"Good." He glances at the clock. "I need another hour in my office, but want to do dinner after?"

"Sure. And if you're looking at endorsement stuff from your agent, be sure to run it by your publicist first." I smirk at him, and he chuckles before he leaves the room.

Before I even get the chance to let that blinking cursor intimidate me some more, someone starts banging on the front door, clearly forgoing the doorbell.

Luke exhales heavily, turns around from the hallway he started down, and moves toward the door instead. He peeks out, and then he opens it.

"You're engaged to my sister?" It's Josh, and he's pissed.

I chuckle from my spot in the kitchen even as I start to realize how big this story is. I've worked with the press before. I know how fast news spreads...I've just never been the subject of that news before.

He comes storming into the kitchen.

"Hey Josh," I say with a wide smile.

He glares at me. "Don't you hey Josh me," he says, pointing a finger in my direction.

Luke rolls his eyes. "Will you please tell your brother that it's all fake?"

My brows dip down. "What's all fake?"

"Our engagement," he says, air quoting the words.

I stand and fold my arms across my chest. "What?" I say sharply. "This is all just fake to you?"

His jaw falls open as he sputters with something to say, and Josh is almost gloating for a beat.

I can't watch Luke sputter any longer. I start laughing. "Yeah, I'm just kidding. It's fake." I slide back into my chair.

Josh sighs. "Why are you doing this?"

I'm not sure if he's asking me or Luke, but Luke fields that one. "It just slipped out when Michelle stopped by. I said we were engaged to get a rise out of her, and your sister very kindly played along. And by the by, Ellie is also handling my PR."

"Nicki mentioned she saw your thirst trap on Instagram," Josh mutters.

"Am I the only one who didn't know what a thirst trap is?" Luke asks.

"Yes," Josh and I say adamantly at the same time.

Luke huffs, and I giggle.

"Who does your social media?" Luke asks my brother.

"Uh, me," Josh says, inflecting his tone at the end to make it sound like he's asking a question. "I may not be the sharpest tool in the shed, but I'm not a complete idiot."

"Apparently I am," Luke says. "Got any more thirsty traps to post?"

"Thirst," I correct.

Josh laughs. "We leave for the airport in a couple hours, but I couldn't leave for three weeks in Fiji without straightening this out first."

"Have a good honeymoon." My eyes return back to my screen.

"Don't forget to pack that really tight and small Speedo you modeled for me," Luke says. "Show off the goods, man."

"Already in the bag," Josh jokes. Then he turns serious for a second. "Before I head out, though, I just want to be clear about one thing." I stop looking at my screen and turn back to my brother. "From where I stand, neither of you is ready to get into a relationship. I know you're faking it or whatever, but just be careful, all right? I don't want to see whatever this is go up in flames because you wanted to help," he says, pointing at me, "and because you took advantage of that." He points at Luke.

"He's not taking advantage," I say. "I volunteered."

"Well that was stupid," Josh says.

"Uh, thanks for your unsolicited opinion." I flash him a sarcastic smile, and he smirks back at me.

"I just care about you both. Have you thought about what happens when Michelle finds out the truth? Won't that give her even more ammo against you, especially if she's really carrying your kid?" he asks Luke.

"For the record, she did send me evidence that she really is knocked up." He holds up a picture of her smiling as she holds a positive pregnancy test toward the camera. "And I haven't thought about her finding out the truth. I guess we'll cross that bridge when we get there."

"You realize you will get there eventually, right?" Josh asks. "At some point, you'll each meet someone and then this arrangement won't work anymore. Or someone will find out the truth. This just isn't a great idea."

We both nod. God, if Josh only knew that Luke and I had sex the night of his bachelor party. I think he'd kill both of us...not that it's really any of his business. I know he's just looking out for the two of us for different reasons, and I know he's coming from a place of love.

But one thing Josh hasn't considered—one thing I've ruminated on pretty much continuously for days—is whether the person I'm supposed to end up with...is Luke.

CHAPTER 3

When I walk into the kitchen the next morning, there's a woman at the stove stirring something in a pot and the kitchen smells like a damn bacon dream.

"You must be Debbie," I say, and the woman turns around with a smile.

"And you must be Ellie," she says. She wipes her hands on her apron and moves around the counter. "Luke told me all about you." She leans forward and gives me a little hug.

"He did?" I ask. What the hell did he say about me?

She smiles. "Congratulations on your engagement. It seems so fast, but Luke's the kind of boy who knows what he wants. I just think it's so sweet that he fell for his best friend's little sister. Isn't that just the thing romance novels are made of?"

So we're faking it even for the house staff. Noted.

"I'm a lucky girl," I say, still wondering exactly what Luke told her about me.

Maybe I need to move bedrooms. Won't it be weird if they're here and see that we're not sleeping together? Is that even something they'd notice, or am I just really searching for ways to sleep with Hot Luke?

And I literally mean *sleep*. Just share a bed.

For now, anyway.

I can't help but wonder what insider info she has on the enigma that is my husband-to-be. How long has she cooked for him? How well does she know him?

"He's outside on the treadmill," she says. "Breakfast should be ready in about ten minutes if you want to let him know."

I nod. "I will. Thanks, Debbie. It's a pleasure to meet you."

"You too," she says, and she gives me a little wink.

I head out to Luke, snap a few more thirst traps that are making me thirsty as all fuck, and chat away while I work.

"Debbie congratulated me," I say.

His lips press together.

I lower my voice. "Are we, um, faking for everyone?"

"I don't know, Ellie." He seems a little frustrated. "I hate lying to people." He slows his running and then stops. He gets off the treadmill and starts stretching. "Maybe we just, I don't know...have a very public break-up or something."

"Yeah," I say softly. "Maybe." I hope not, especially not after I put out a press release this morning where Luke takes full responsibility for the baby and also full responsibility for his own happiness.

I head back inside because Luke is crabby. Maybe he just needs some of Debbie's home cooking to cheer him up.

"Is Luke taking you to the ball tomorrow night?" Debbie asks.

Ball?

What ball?

I don't say that. In fact, I don't know *what* to say. I'm about to stammer out some non-response when he walks in.

"Debbie was just asking me about tomorrow night's ball," I say to him, my eyes wide as if to ask him *what ball is this and why didn't you mention it and are we going* all in one look.

Clearly we're not at the place where he can read my nonverbal communication.

"I was planning on skipping it," he says.

"Why?" Debbie asks. "Aren't they expecting you?"

He nods. "Yeah, but I don't have a..." he trails off as his eyes widen, and I'm pretty sure he was about to end that sentence with *date*.

He's really *not* a good liar.

"Tux," he finishes. "My, uh, tux isn't clean."

"Oh, Luke, I can take care of that for you," Debbie says.

Luke blows out a breath. "You're not letting me get out of this one, are you?"

She shoots him a smirk. "Nope."

I stand and look back and forth between the two of them, a little unsure as to whether I should admit I have no idea what ball they're talking about. And then Luke fills in the blanks for me.

"Would you be my date for the seventh annual Beating Hunger in Vegas Charity Ball?" he asks.

"I'd love to," I say. "And, for the record, this is one of those amazing opportunities to post on your social media."

And then I do a mini-freak out on the inside.

Hot Luke just asked me out on a date.

Okay, okay...so he was kind of forced into it, and we're putting on an act...but still.

We're going to a charity ball together.

Tomorrow night.

Oh shit. I need to find a dress and shoes and figure out what the hell to do with my hair.

"Social media?" Debbie asks. "Like Facebook?"

I nod. "I got him all set up."

"She's doing some public relations stuff for me."

Debbie beams as she looks between the two of us. "Oh my goodness, Luke. I already *love* her for you."

He laughs as my insides warm. "Ellie, I know it's short notice for the ball, and I'm sorry about that. But don't worry. We'll get it all sorted."

We better. That's all I have to say about that.

Debbie leaves not too long after that, and my questions start immediately over a pancake and bacon plus Lucky Charms breakfast at the kitchen table instead of the counter, where we usually eat our meals.

That's right. I have a *routine* with Hot Luke.

"Okay, first things first," I say. "Lucky Charms *again*?"

He shrugs. "Get used to it. It's my personal obsession."

"Noted. Second, Debbie thinks we're engaged. Does the rest of your house staff know? And is it weird that we sleep in separate bedrooms?"

He glances up at me. "Yeah, I've been thinking about that, too." He looks down at his plate. "We should probably just move you into my room for now unless that's too weird for you."

"It's fine," I say maybe just a tad too quickly. "Next, what the hell am I supposed to wear to the ball tomorrow night? The bridesmaid's dress I ruined when I fell in the pool?"

He laughs. "You can borrow my card and take it shopping. Get whatever you want. Dress, shoes, jewelry. I don't care."

Okay...well that sounds like fun.

After we clean up the breakfast dishes, Luke says, "Should we move your stuff into my room?"

I shrug even though my heart is beating in triple time at the thought of actually sleeping beside this man. I didn't even get to do that the night we had sex since he bolted so fast. At least now I know the reason for the bolting was Pepper, not me.

We each grab a load of clothes from my room and walk down the hallway toward the double doors of the master bedroom, and my heart races as I realize this is the very first time I'm seeing his bedroom even though I've lived here for the last four days.

He opens the doors.

His bedroom is masculine. The bed linens are a charcoal gray, the furniture is dark wood, and one entire wall is made up of a puzzle of reclaimed wood. It's the perfect backdrop for more thirst traps. And while I liked the view from my bedroom, the windows in here are much larger and offer a gorgeous view of the mountains and the Las Vegas Strip off in the distance beyond my brother's house.

It's incredible.

It's sexy.

It's luxurious.

And, for now, even if it's pretend...it's mine.

He takes me through an expansive bathroom and into his closet, which is neat as a pin and larger than the bedroom in the apartment I lived in back in Chicago. His clothes are mostly black, white, and gray, with the odd splash of red here and there to represent the Aces team colors, black and red. A huge, framed Aces jersey rests on one wall with DALTON and the number eighty-four on it. His clothes only take up one side of the closet. The other side is completely empty, almost like he was waiting for someone...waiting for me.

He nods to some drawers built into the wall. "You can put your stuff in those drawers. They're all empty."

I want to ask why they're empty, but I have a feeling I know the answer. When Savannah moved out and then Michelle, he just never refilled them. He probably never needed to. His side of the closet is fairly sparsely used, so there was no need to change up his system of organization.

Sort of like the bathroom, which I find also has empty drawers just waiting for my stuff.

After I fill the drawers, I glance at the bed as I think about what *could* happen in there versus what likely *will* happen.

Being around him is almost too much for me as it is. And now he's going to be sleeping mere inches away from me in the same bed every single night.

This is going to be the most beautifully difficult situation I've ever found myself in.

"Fuck," he mutters, clicking something on his phone.

"What?"

He collapses on the bed and heaves out a sigh, and then he holds his phone up for me to take. I read the headline on his screen.

Is Dalton Lying? His New Fiancée's Ex Spills the Tea.

It's from some celebrity gossip vlog, and I click to watch the video. "Billy Peters here with your latest *Celebrity Snaps*!"

I raise a brow over the phone as I look at Luke. "Looks like someone thinks athletes are celebrities."

He chuckles even though this isn't funny.

"Breaking news, gossip mongers," the flamboyant host declares on the screen. "Sin City is heating up and not just from the sunshine. The Luke Dalton scandal is full of all the tea, and I'm here to spill it today."

He snaps his fingers and the screen flips to a photo of Luke in his football uniform. And *fuck* does he look delicious.

"Hottie football star Dalton knocked up his ex and then got engaged to another woman. His press release from this morning makes it sound like he'll be there for the ex while he's planning his wedding to the woman he loves—side note, his *teammate's sister*—but...are you ready for this tea?" He pauses, and the picture flips to an image of a fish. "Something's fishy!"

It flips back to the host. "Luke's new fiancée split from her ex *less than a week ago*. He's claiming there's no way she could be engaged already." He makes a huge round O shape with his mouth. "Somebody's lying! Stay tuned for all the latest on this juicy tale."

The video cuts there, and I blink at the screen.

Fucking Todd.

I heave out a breath. "I'm sorry," I mutter.

"For what?" he asks.

"For dating that douche-bucket in the first place."

Luke laughs.

"How can you laugh at a time like this?"

He sits up and lifts a shoulder. "Douche-bucket." He chuckles again. "What else can we do? We can laugh or we can commiserate. I choose laughter. And then we take action, right?"

I nod, and then an idea forms.

Take action.

I draw in a deep breath as a lightbulb seems to click on over my head. When he first mentioned it, my initial reaction was hell to the no. But now...

I lift a shoulder. "Maybe we should just get married. That would shut up Todd *and* Michelle."

He freezes. Then, as if moving in slow motion, he looks up at me. "What?"

"Let's just get married. We're in *Vegas*. It's like the land of quickie weddings, isn't it?"

He narrows his eyes. "You didn't seem too into the idea when I first mentioned it."

"I wasn't," I admit. I'd always planned to get married only once in my life. In fact, as someone who fully believes in fairy tales, I admit that marriage is both serious and sacred to me, yet something about doing this with Luke seems right.

I want to help him even though I've only known him for a few days. I have these urges to protect him and I don't even know why. My body knows his body, and that's a language the two of us were fluent in that one night. My heart has been introduced to his heart.

I fully expect this *marriage* sham will only last a few months, maybe a year. But I'm at a point in my life where it's one adventure after another, and what bigger adventure could I embark upon right now other than dedicating my entire life to becoming a football wife? I'm already devoting a huge chunk of my time to this man as his public relations manager. Why not just take it another step (okay, a few thousand steps) further?

At the worst, it's maybe a year out of my life. Even if Luke and I end up hating one another, if we agree to just one year, he has a big enough house that we could basically avoid each other. I could go live in the damn pool house if I need to. And there's a lot of potential in that it might open doors for my career. It might give me a whole new network of people— *celebrities*, which, I'll admit now, even includes athletes—to meet and potentially work with.

"I've got nothing else going on," I say instead of any of that, and I realize it makes me sound both desperate and incredibly sad.

He presses his lips together. "I had a hard enough time coming to terms with you agreeing to be my fake fiancée. But my fake wife?" He shakes his head and glances away from me. "When I said it at first, it just sort of slipped out. But I just...I don't see myself getting married again. Not after Savannah destroyed me the way she did."

I nod even though I feel a little defeated. He's the one who brought it up first. "Okay. It was a stupid idea. Forget it."

He drums his fingers on the table beside him where he stands, and then he heaves out a huge breath. "What if it's not a stupid idea? Am I stupid for actually considering it?"

My brows shoot up. "You're considering it?"

"Josh will kill us both."

"This isn't about my brother," I say. "I don't really care what his opinion is. If I'm in and you're in, isn't that all that matters?"

He nods. "I don't know if I'm in."

"Okay, so we're trial running me as your PR manager for the next week or two, right? What if we trial run me as your fiancée, too?"

He nods and steeples his fingers in front of his mouth. "Okay, I like where your head's at, but what do *you* get out of it?"

"I get to be married to a hot ass football star."

He laughs and shakes his head modestly and with a touch of embarrassment. "I'm insane for even considering this," he breathes, and he pauses. "You'd need to get something out of it. I could double what I offered to pay you for my PR. And, no offense, we'd need an airtight prenup. I don't know you well enough to fork over half of everything I own when we know there's an end date on it."

I pretend his words don't kill a little piece of me. I fully know what I'm getting myself into here. I'm under no illusion that he'll magically fall in love with me and we'll navigate our very own fairy tale as we find our way to our happily ever after.

Even though a girl can still hope and dream.

CHAPTER 4

Luke's watching ESPN to catch today's sports highlights while I flip through the selection of dresses on the mobile sites of some local stores, and then he clicks for the recorded shows on his DVR and starts a football game.

It's the Aces against the Bears. I glance over at him with pursed lips, and he laughs at my expression.

"Listen, babe. If you're engaged to me, you better understand the basics of what I do." He clicks a button on the remote.

I huff out an annoyed breath and give him a look with raised brows. I hold out my hand toward the television as if to say, *all right, let's get on with it.*

"Lesson one," he begins. "This is just a quick overview of the game."

He starts telling me about quarters and downs and yardage and blitzes, and the way he's so passionate as he talks is both endearing and incredibly sexy. He clearly *loves* the game. He loves what he does, and as he shows me examples of each part of the game he explains, I actually start to get it.

All the times Josh and my dad have tried to explain this damn game to me were absolute failures. But after one session with Luke, I finally understand what a first down is.

I even know the little thing the fans do with their arms to indicate a first down.

I see him in his uniform. I watch for number eighty-four. I see him catch the ball. I see him *run*.

It's really freaking hot.

He's fast and agile, and watching him play the sport that's everything to him sort of peels back another layer of who he is. I can see it in the way his eyes study the screen before they light with passion when he glances at me to explain what something means. I can hear it in the inflection of his voice, both excited to talk about the game and patient as he explains what must be the most rudimentary aspects of it.

He *loves* this game. It's the most important thing in his life.

I get why he's scared going into the last year of his contract. He doesn't know what comes next because he's never really had to think about it. He's been too busy living his dream to worry about the next stage even though it looms closer and closer every season.

It's not just that, though. He's not just looming closer to the end of his career...but he's doing it *alone*. When he got married, surely he didn't expect to get divorced. Nobody goes into marriage with that mindset—unless you're doing it as a sham, I guess. He must've seen her in his future so that when his career was over, he'd have someone there beside him as he entered into whatever phase of life came after the game.

And maybe that's why I fell into his life. Maybe part of my job here isn't just to help him continue playing for the team he loves so damn much. Maybe it's also helping him discover what the next phase of his life is going to be once it's time to transition...because that time *will* come whether he's ready for it or not. He can't play football *forever*.

I can't help my yawn as the clock strikes eleven.

"Sorry," Luke says, his eyes still animated as he watches the game. "I'm boring you now."

I laugh. "Actually, not at all. I could listen to you talk about football forever." I realize how much I mean those words when they tumble out of my mouth. Watching how excited he gets about a catch is something lovely to behold. "It's just getting late."

He glances at the clock. "Yeah. Sorry, I get caught up when I'm talking about the game. You ready to go to bed?"

I nod. It's our first night sharing a bed, and that thought is a little daunting. "I think I'll head up."

"You go ahead," he says. "I'm just going to watch a little more film."

"Film?" I ask.

He chuckles. "It's just what we call it. An older word leftover from another time. I'm going to watch a little more of this game and study it. Look at what I did, what I could have done differently, what those around me and on the other side of the ball did, that sort of thing."

"Okay," I say, and I have this strange and totally natural urge to lean over to kiss him goodnight. But I don't. I somehow stop myself. "Have fun watching your film."

His laughter follows me out of the room, and I'm kind of glad that I'm heading to bed first tonight. That way I can pretend to be asleep when he comes in because I sure as hell know I'll be too nervous to actually fall asleep as I'm just lying there waiting for him.

I get ready for bed, and then I stand in front of the mattress as I realize we didn't pick *sides* when we talked about this arrangement. I assume he'll want the side the clock is on, so I go to the other side. I don't use a bedside clock since I sleep with my phone next to me. Maybe he's old school with this whole clock thing he's got going on. I snap the light off and slide down into the bed.

It's fucking luxurious. The sheets must be a billion-thread count, and the mattress is firm and cool.

His sheets smell like him, and suddenly I'm incredibly horny lying in the bed of the man I'm crushing *hard* on.

Okay, maybe not *suddenly*, but smelling him as the cool sheets lie over my body is making the ache between my thighs rage for him.

I'm just about to dip my fingers into my panties to find some tiny measure of relief when his bedroom door opens.

He's quiet as he closes it behind him, shutting himself into the dark room. He uses the flashlight on his phone to move around the room, and I lie as still as I can, my hand resting just under the elastic band of my panties.

He disappears into the bathroom, and I ease my fingers out before I get caught.

That was close.

I probably shouldn't even consider fingering myself in someone else's bed.

But he just...does that to me. He makes me want to make bad decisions.

He's only in the bathroom a few minutes before he emerges and slides quietly into the bed beside me. I force my breathing to stay even because I don't know what the hell to say to him. We're sharing a bed. It's all for pretend. My massive crush on him seems to be getting exponentially larger by the millisecond, but it doesn't matter because he's already written me off.

I'm sure he thinks I'm fast asleep.

And then he whispers into the darkness. "Sweet dreams, Sexy Ellie."

Oh, that's just great.

One more thing for my overactive brain to overanalyze.

Long GAME

I must fall asleep at some point because when I open my eyes to the bright morning, Luke isn't in bed. He's an early bird, obviously, and he's already catching the worm.

Except when I glance at my phone, I see that I've slept in...and I have a missed call and voicemail from my mother.

It's already nine—later than usual for me, but I was up pretty late trying to figure out why he'd call me Sexy Ellie when he's made it so clear that he doesn't want to be with me. What a confusing guy.

I blow out a breath as I click through to my mother's voicemail. I'm not looking forward to this already.

"Ellie Marie Nolan, how in the world could you get *engaged* and not even tell your mother? What is going on with you? How well do you even know this guy? You've only been there a few days! Are you crazy? Are you pregnant? Is it Todd's? Am I going to be a grandmother? Call me!"

She's a handful.

And I'm neither caffeinated nor drunk enough to answer any of her questions. Not any of the fifteen thousand of them.

Instead, I take a shower and head down for breakfast. I slept too late to catch the morning show better known as Hot Luke's Workout, but he's just coming in from the patio, a towel around his neck and his skin glistening with sweat. His hair is wet and his face is flushed and his abs are practically calling my name but I'm apparently not allowed to answer that call.

"My, uh, mom called," I say, trying my damnedest not to be distracted by those abs. I'm trying not to even think about them, but it's impossible. The more I try not to, the more the only thing I can think of is them. My eyes flick down of their own accord, and when they wander back up to meet Luke's, his are a little heated...and not from the workout. At least I don't think that's what it's from. I've been wrong about these things before, though. "It seems she saw our news. Are we keeping the lie up to our families—apart from Josh since he already knows—or do they get the truth?"

Luke sighs and glances away from me before he answers. "I'm not telling my family but I'm not going to tell you what to do with yours."

I nod. "Okay. Can I ask why?"

"My brother will go straight to the press and blow our whole cover." He glances away from me like he's hiding his true emotions about all that.

We may not have known each other long yet, but I *will* find a way to get him to open up. He doesn't need to screen his emotions around me.

"Do you have any other siblings?" I ask.

Pepper walks over to Luke with a ball in her mouth and drops it at his feet. He tosses it into the family room, and she runs to get it. "Yeah, a sister, Kaylee. She's still in college. She was a surprise ten years after I came along."

"Are you close with your siblings?"

He lifts a shoulder. "Not really. I really only see them on our annual family trip."

"How come?" I ask.

"We don't see each other on the traditional holidays because my brother and I can't make it. I talk to my parents maybe once every three or four months. Jack and I occasionally shoot off a football-related text to each other. Kaylee texts me a few times a week." He shrugs with nonchalance, like it's not a big deal he isn't close with his family when to me that's a totally foreign concept.

"Is that hard?" I ask, and I move toward the fridge.

"It's actually easier that way." He leaves it at that, and I don't press despite the strong desire to.

I look in the refrigerator and find some little egg muffins Debbie left. I take two and put them on a plate. "The annual family trip sounds fun."

"It's fine." He nods at my egg muffins. "Can you make me two of those?" Pepper returns and he tosses the ball again while I arrange more on the plate, and then he walks over to the pantry and grabs the box of Lucky Charms. "It's always nice to escape the Vegas heat in the middle of summer."

I'm about to ask a follow up on the weather when I realize that's exactly how Luke manages to keep himself private and why I've been living with him for a week now and I still don't know much about him. He brings up topics that we can explore in our conversation that have nothing to do with him. I can look up the weather later.

What I can't look up is Luke Dalton.

Although the thirst traps have been working. His Instagram account is building quickly, and I can tell his fans want more.

Even though a tiny part of me wants to keep him all to myself.

That's not what he's paying me to do, though.

"Where do you take your family trips?" I ask after I stick the plate in the microwave.

"Always somewhere different, and we rotate who picks the location. Last year my brother chose New Zealand."

"Oh wow. How was it?" I grab another plate and some forks.

"It should have been amazing, but Michelle was there." He pours himself a bowl of cereal and holds it up in my direction as if to ask if I'd like some. I shake my head, and then he mutters, "She managed to find ways to make it miserable."

"What about this year?" I ask.

"Kaylee has chosen Hawaii."

"Mm," I murmur. "That sounds nice. Where was your pick?"

"Two years ago we did an Alaskan cruise." He grabs some juice from the fridge and holds it up in my direction. "Want some?"

I nod. "How was that?"

"Same answer as New Zealand." He fills two cups as he talks. "My family didn't care for her, so it ended up not being a very family-oriented trip, which is sort of the whole point."

The microwave beeps, and I take out the muffins. I arrange two on a plate for myself and meet Luke on the other side of the counter. "I bet this year you're looking forward to Hawaii without Michelle and just your family," I muse.

His answer shocks me.

Shock isn't a strong enough word.

I'm fucking obliterated.

"Just my family and my fiancée."

My jaw falls open dumbly, and I can't seem to form words.

"Yeah." He nods and gives a little laugh as he elbows my arm. "That's you."

"You want *me* to come to *Hawaii* with you on your *family* trip at the end of this month?" This is his *family* trip. The one he takes annually. The only chance he gets to see his family each year.

And he wants me to come? Why? To keep up the ruse?

His brows raise and he presses his lips together and nods. "That about sums up our conversation. It's on me if you want to go. We'd probably have nice backdrops for your hungry traps."

"Thirst traps," I murmur, but is he for real offering me a free trip to Hawaii where I'll spend days upon days with *his entire family*? I'm floored. And I'm nervous. I know literally nothing about his family other than the fact that he and his brother have some intense sibling rivalry.

"Is that a yes?" he asks.

"Oh my God, Luke!" I toss my arms around his neck and press a kiss to his mouth without even thinking twice about it. He's hot and sweaty but I could not care less. I'm crushed against Luke Dalton and it's exactly where I want to be. He presses his fingers to my hips for just a beat like he's about to give into this pull between the two of us...but then he backs away. He chuckles, and my cheeks burn. "Yes it's a yes!"

They're the only words I can think to say after I just totally embarrassed myself by kissing him, but I try to play it like it was a thank you kiss.

Though that does beg the question of what I'll be willing to do as a thank you when he actually takes me on the trip. There's not much that wouldn't be on that list, if you catch my drift.

"Do you have any champagne?" I ask after we sit and start eating.

"To celebrate your upcoming trip to Hawaii?"

I shake my head. "Mimosas are one of the few acceptable breakfast drinks, and I'm gonna need a little something before I call my mom back."

He laughs. "Is she really that bad?" He stands and walks over to one of the lower cabinets near the refrigerator. He opens the cabinet door to reveal a wine cooler. He grabs a bottle, pops the cork, and hands it over.

"Thanks," I say. "Impressive little wine refrigerator."

He laughs. "It's a wine *cooler* and a complete beverage center, actually."

"You drink a lot of wine?"

He shakes his head. "Next to never. Beer or whiskey for me. But I keep a stock of it for entertaining. Now tell me about your mom."

I let that *entertaining* comment slide even though I want to know if it's because he has big parties or if it's because he's entertaining different *women*. I hope it's not a wide variety of women...but I also remember my brother was working hard to get him laid the night of the bachelor party, so maybe not any recent conquests. At least I hope not.

I brush those thoughts away and heave in a breath as I think about my mom. She's equal parts critical and loving mixed with a little old-fashioned.

"She's a handful. She usually means well enough, but let's just say Josh is her favorite and I'm the disappointment."

"I doubt that," he says softly, and then he dumps some champagne into his orange juice, too.

"He gets a pass on everything. When Todd dumped me, her first words were literally about how she's going to have to wait even longer for grandchildren when her son was getting married a few days later. Can't he produce grandchildren?" I say it lightly because it's just the way she is. I'm not damaged or scarred from it, and if anything, it's a big joke between my brother and me—something that, over the years, has drawn us closer if nothing else than for the laughs.

"If it makes you feel any better, my brother is my dad's favorite and my sister is my mom's favorite. I'm just on a lonely island," he says. He flashes me a smirk, and we don't dig further into it even though I want to know why he hid behind the smirk.

After breakfast, I finally make the call to my mom—even though the champagne wasn't nearly strong enough.

And I lie through my teeth—the same damn lie we'll be telling everyone.

She buys it.

This might be easier than we think.

CHAPTER 5

I stare at myself in the mirror.

I found the perfect dress exactly three minutes after I walked into the first store, and they had shoes and jewelry that work as the perfect accessories. The dress fits like it was made for me. His tux is black so I had a pretty wide palette of colors to choose from. I settled on a gorgeous purple that makes my skin glow. I took an hour to curl my hair into loose waves that cascade around my shoulders, and I spent extra time perfecting my make-up. I feel like a different person.

I feel like the future wife of a football player.

I glance at the clock and see that I'm officially out of time. Luke wanted to leave no later than six forty-five, and that gives me two minutes to get downstairs where he's already waiting for me.

I move toward the top of the stairs and start my descent made a little slower in these tall heels. I'll get used to them—I hope. I think back to what happened at the wedding.

God, please don't let me fall into any pools tonight.

When I walk into the kitchen, Luke looks up, and our eyes meet.

My heart races.

His dark eyes sweep along my entire form, and I grip onto the counter because I feel like my knees might buckle at the sight of Hot Luke in his hot tux.

He looks much the same as he did at my brother's wedding in a different tux less than a full week ago, yet at the same time...he looks totally different to me.

He looks like a man I could potentially fall for. A man I *am* falling for. Every second we spend together, another little piece of me belongs to him.

And I'm afraid the more time I spend with him, the more I'm going to keep falling. Then what? What happens once I'm done falling and I'm already there...but he isn't?

I force the thought away.

I have to. I can't go into a night like tonight and play the part with those thoughts plaguing me. But it's still a very real and very scary concern.

"Wow," he says softly, and he takes a step toward me. He reaches around my waist and pulls me into him. I grip onto his bicep. It's hard and freaking huge and I need to keep holding on or I might fall over. "You look beautiful."

My heart hammers and my stomach flips being so close to him. I breathe in the same cologne he wore at the wedding—something he doesn't wear every day, just for special occasions. It's a little peek into who he is, and it makes me want more. It makes me *crave* more. I want to know *everything* about this man. What he likes, what he dislikes, what makes him tick, what makes him smile.

What makes him moan.

And maybe I'll get that chance.

It certainly feels like I could when I'm this close to him.

I close my eyes and breathe him in.

He presses a soft kiss to my cheek, the dark scruff on his jaw scratching my face and forcing memories of our single night together back to the surface of my mind. I want him to kiss me. I want his mouth on mine. I want all of him wanting all of me again.

"Our ride is waiting out front," Luke says, breaking up the intimate trance we find ourselves in.

I follow him to the front door, and he asks, "Is purple your favorite color?"

"Yeah," I murmur.

"It looks nice on you," he says softly, and then he locks the front door before he helps me into the backseat then gets in on the other side. His eyes meet mine once he shuts the door, and a little heat passes between us before he looks away first.

He's not in the right place to get into a relationship, and especially not with someone who wants the fairy tale ending. I have to keep reminding myself of that...but when he looks at me the way he just did, I have to wonder *why*.

We're quiet in the car on the way to the event—or rather *he* is quiet and I'm wrestling with what to say the whole way. I finally break the silence with a question. "Will any of your teammates be there?"

He shrugs. "Yeah, there will probably be at least a few guys there. Any big ticket event like this one always has local celebrities. I wasn't planning on going so I didn't ask around."

"We should have snapped a few pics by your pool before we left," I muse. More thirst traps with this guy in a tux. "Well, if you're ready to unveil me as your fiancée."

"I think we're past the point of whether I'm ready," he says dryly.

Twenty minutes later, we pull up to the venue and the driver lets us out. Other couples dressed like we are emerge from similar chauffeured cars and walk through the doors presumably for the same event we're attending.

I feel out of place as soon as we walk into the room after we check in and receive our dinner table number. My arm is firmly planted through his, and that seems to be about the only thing keeping me steady at the moment.

I recognize faces I've seen before just about everywhere I look. An actor here. A television host there. A famous singer here. A model there. Some seem to know Luke, friendly greetings and head nods going back and forth, and I feel even further out of my element.

I grip onto Luke's arm a little more tightly, and I almost feel like he's holding a little more tightly onto me, too. It must be my imagination.

I'm just a normal girl, a public relations manager from Chicago, and suddenly I'm on the arm of a very handsome man as his fiancée at a fancy soiree where the dinner plates cost upward of a few hundred dollars. Maybe even a thousand. I haven't gotten up the nerve to ask, and I won't.

But this whole event is to raise money, so I'm sure it didn't come cheap.

"So you paid for two dinners and you just…weren't going to show up?" I ask under my breath as I look around the classy room and the elegant people moving about it.

He lifts a shoulder. "I wrote it off as a donation."

I glance over at him, and he looks stiff. Uncomfortable.

Out of his element, too.

"Are you okay?" I ask.

He tugs at his collar and clears his throat. "These events aren't my thing. Savannah forced me to go to the first one with her because she liked rubbing elbows with the rich and famous."

"Have you come every year?"

He nods as we stop in a short line near a bar. "This was the first I was planning to miss, actually." He glances down at me, and I try to figure out what's in his gaze. I don't know him well enough yet to interpret it.

"I'm glad we came," I say softly.

One side of his mouth tips into a smile, and then it's our turn to order. He opts for beer, and I order some wine. We keep it simple, and I start to feel an idea forming as I watch him tug at his collar again.

I need Luke to do more for the community, but I want him in a setting where he feels comfortable. The idea hasn't quite formed yet. It's just the start of the snowfall, but I feel like it might be starting to roll into something that resembles a snowman.

"Dalton!" a deep voice behind us says.

We both turn around, and I see someone who looks familiar. I think he might've been one of the groomsmen at my brother's wedding, but let's face it, I sort of had tunnel vision for Luke so I can't really be positive on that one.

"Fletcher!" Luke says in the same tone of voice. "I didn't know you'd be here."

"And yet here I am." He flashes Luke a smile and then his eyes edge over to me.

"This is Ellie," Luke says. "Ellie, this is Brandon Fletcher."

"Nice to meet you," I say, sticking out my hand, and he gives me a look like we've met before.

"You're Nolan's sister," he says, and I nod.

"And my future wife," Luke adds.

Brandon's brows both shoot up. "Your *future wife*?" He doesn't hide his shock for my benefit. "I didn't even know you were dating anybody since that train wreck with Michelle."

Luke shrugs. "We've known each other a while and the timing was just never right." He glances at me, and hot damn he's a good actor because hell if I don't see all the adoration in his eyes that I'd expect him to have when he's looking at his fiancée. "And then it was, and now here we are."

"Well congrats, man," Brandon says, slapping him on the back.

Luke presses his lips together in one of those *thanks* sort of smiles.

"When's the wedding?"

Luke and I exchange a glance, and I field this one. "We just got engaged, so we haven't had time to plan anything yet."

"Before camp, though, right? I'd love to get fucked up on your dime." Brandon booms out a laugh, and I gather that he plays for the Aces, too.

Luke offers a casual shrug. "We haven't made any decisions yet." It's both the closest to the truth and the easiest way to get out of committing to anything.

A beautiful woman with really huge boobs saunters up beside Brandon. She practically hangs herself on him, clearly proving that she's here with him and he's going home with her.

Okay, honey, we get it. He's your guy.

"This is Lauren," he says, nodding to the woman without really looking at her or acknowledging her. "My date," he adds, and the way he says it tells me that she's way more invested in whatever is going on between the two of them than he is.

We wait for them to order their drinks, and as they order, Luke quietly informs me that Brandon is the quarterback for the Aces.

I should probably have known that considering my brother plays for the team and my future husband does, too, and I've even watched *film* with Luke...but I didn't.

Once they get their drinks, we mingle around the room with them. We run into one of the defensive coaches and some other people he knows, and Luke introduces me to everyone as his *future wife*.

I guess that makes it pretty official.

And then we run into an older man who looks like he bleeds money.

Long GAME

"Mr. Dalton," he says. He side-eyes me, and Luke seems suddenly nervous—quite a different look than I'm used to on the guy with all the confidence I've started getting to know.

"Mr. Bennett," he says, and he turns to me. "This is Ellie Nolan. Ellie, meet Mr. Calvin Bennett, the owner of the Vegas Aces."

Okay, now I get it. He's nervous because he's worried about his future with the Aces. He's scared that the younger players are going to replace him, and the owner is the one who gets the final say in all that. That's basically the highest boss at his company…if you don't count the fans.

"Mr. Bennet, lovely to meet you," I say, reaching out a hand to shake his.

He nods once. "You're Josh Nolan's sister and Luke's fiancée," he says. Yeah, I'm aware of that, thanks. I'm not sure where he's going with that until he delivers his next sentence. "You're connected to more than one of my men."

I give him my warmest smile, and Luke blanches. I reach over and squeeze Luke's hand in solidarity. "I am. And I love them both so much." I give him a giggle. "In very different ways, obviously."

I glance over at Luke, who looks like he wants to be anywhere but here, and then Calvin's smiling eyes turn a little serious as they edge to my future husband. "Luke, we need to talk. I'll expect you in my office Monday morning, and I'll expect the press taken care of by then. Remember where your priorities are."

Luke nods. "Yes, sir. You know where my top priority is."

Calvin gives him a long stare, and I almost think for a second that he's about to say something more. Maybe something about how families should be his top priority…that football is important, obviously, but that as long as his head's on straight where the game is concerned, maybe other things—particularly in the offseason—can also be priorities in his life.

They're not, for the record, and I can't help but think that maybe that's another part of the reason he's had two failed relationships in the last few years. You know, in addition to the fact that the women he chose were nightmares.

But he doesn't say any of that. Instead, he simply nods and moves along to a different conversation, and Luke lets out a breath with a muttered curse as he guides me to our table.

"What does he need to talk to you about?" I ask. "The baby headline?" I can't imagine why he'd really care about that. I'm sure football players have done far worse than impregnating one woman when they're about to marry another, but I guess I can kind of see how Luke's behavior might reflect poorly on the organization as a whole.

Luke clears his throat, and he looks a little pale as he glances over at me.

"Hey, are you okay?" I ask, reaching over to squeeze his hand.

He shrugs. "I could fucking kill Michelle and Savannah for that goddamn article, but yeah, I'm okay."

"Your boss seems..."

"Nice?" he deadpans, and I chuckle.

"He seems like he really cares about you guys."

He raises a brow at me as he pulls out my chair. "You got that from what he said to me?"

I take my seat, and Brandon immediately pulls his attention so I don't get to answer, and then the first of our seven courses is served.

We listen to the keynote speaker during our dessert, and then we're told that the dance floor is open.

Lauren drags Brandon out there, who looks helplessly at Luke and flags his hands in the *come here* signal.

Luke laughs. "Care to dance?" he asks me.

"I'd love to," I say, and the truth is there's no way in hell I'm missing my chance to get closer to Luke Dalton.

The first song is a faster dance song, and Luke seems uncomfortable. It transitions into a slower song, and he looks awkwardly at me. I lift a shoulder and smile as an invitation to let him know it's okay to dance, and he smiles back before he takes me in his arms.

My body is crushed to his. My heart races, and my legs turn to jelly as I breathe him in.

There's nothing I want more than for all of this to be real.

"The only reason he's even dancing with her is because he knows it's his ticket to getting laid," he says softly to me.

I giggle.

"Is that why you're dancing with me?" I ask.

His eyes flash with some hot combination of danger and slyness. "That night was certainly something."

I want him to say more. It was *certainly something*? Does this guy, like, *rehearse* lines that he can throw at me that'll cause me to overanalyze and overthink them later?

"Yeah," I murmur. "Something..." I trail off, leaving the door open for him.

"You know how I felt about it," he says softly.

Do I, though?

Not really.

I lean back and look in his eyes to say just that, but more heat passes between us and my train of thought goes off the rails. I think he's about to lean in to kiss me, but then he doesn't.

He heaves out a sigh. "God, I hate tuxes." He yanks at the neck of his shirt again.

I clear my throat. "So if you could hold a charity event, it wouldn't be black tie with a seven course meal and after dinner dancing?"

He shakes his head. "Fuck no. It would be casual. People would be encouraged to show up in running shorts and t-shirts. There would be a buffet table with appetizers and another with desserts and you could dance if you want but it would be because you're drunk."

And that's when the snowflake from earlier forms right into that snowman in my mind. "Oh my God," I murmur. "That's it!"

"What's it?" His brows dip down and he looks epically confused.

"A charity event. Hosted by you. Casual, fun, beer, running shorts. It can be whatever you want it to be, and it's the perfect start to get you moving in the community like we talked about."

He tilts his head a little as he thinks over the idea. "But I don't have time to plan an event."

My face is the picture of sarcasm for a second, but I force my wrinkled brow and twisted mouth straight again. "Okay, well it seems like you have a bunch of free time right now in the offseason to plan something, but whatever. I can do it, or we can hire somebody."

He chuckles. "Okay, so then what would I even do? What charity would it be for?"

"What's important to you?" I ask.

His shrugs as he thinks, and then he says, "I'd want to help either dogs or kids."

"There are tons of things you can do for kids. You can create your own charity for whatever's important to you. Or you can give back to someone else. There are charities for kids who are sick, for foster kids, for dropout prevention, for spending time with kids, for granting wishes, for sex trafficking, for drug abuse, for helping those in poor communities, for building playgrounds..."

I trail off as that last one seems to spark an idea in his eyes.

"Building playgrounds?"

I nod. "I worked with a charity in Chicago where they refurbished and modernized old playgrounds to make them usable for kids again. Is that something important to you?"

The song changes and it's another slow one, so we keep moving together as we have what feels like an important conversation.

"Something close to that," he says. "I was always outside when I was a kid. I've thought about doing something to help build athletic fields in the community. As part of that, though, I also want to create a scholarship fund for young kids whose parents can't afford to put them in sports." His eyes start to light with the fire of passion as he talks.

"I love that idea," I say, and my arms tighten a little around his neck. It's an involuntary move, almost like I'm hugging him while we're dancing, and his fingertips press into my back, sending flutters right through my stomach. "I think it totally fits who you are while it also gives you the chance to do something positive here in the community. And not just for the media attention you'll get, but because it's something you're passionate about."

He looks thoughtful for a beat. "Let's look into it. So I have the idea for what I'd want to do to help the community, but what kind of event would we do?" He glances around and lowers his voice. "It can't be like this. It's not me."

I laugh. "So you've indicated. I don't know, what would be a fun event? You could do a celebrity softball tournament, or one of those football games where you just mess around for fun—what's that called?"

His brows dip down. "Scrimmage?"

"Yeah, that."

He laughs. "But I thought you said athletes weren't celebrities."

I lift a shoulder. "I stand by that."

He laughs again.

"I'm kidding. I didn't mean for it to sound how it sounded when I said that. You just...I don't know. You make me nervous," I admit.

"I make you nervous?" he asks, a sly little smile playing at his lips. My eyes flick there for a beat and between his lips and how fantastic he smells, my knees nearly give out on me.

I nod. "Incredibly."

"Huh," he says in wonder, and my eyes move back to his. "That's interesting because the feeling's sort of mutual."

My tummy somersaults as he holds my gaze for a beat longer than we should as *friends*.

But we're not friends...not really. I'm working for him. I'm his fake fiancée. I'm his roommate. I'm his best friend's little sister. At this point, we hardly know each other, but I'm getting to know him. And every new piece of Hot Luke that I discover presses my feelings for him just a little deeper.

He clears his throat. "Cornhole."

His single word breaks the daze I started falling into.

"Um...excuse me?"

"Cornhole," he repeats, like I just didn't hear him the first time. No, I definitely heard him, but what the fuck is cornhole? Is he...

No. I shake off the thought.

Wait a minute.

Is he offering me butt play?

"Right. Okay." I nod like I get it.

"You have no idea what cornhole is, do you?" he says, and it sounds less like a question and more like a statement.

"No," I lie, because I'm pretty sure a cornhole is a butthole. "Not a clue."

He laughs. "It's a game where you have two wooden platforms placed a certain distance apart and they have holes in the top of them. Then you throw beanbags and try to get them into the hole. That could be my charity event. Celebrity cornhole."

"Oh!" I say, a little flustered that I thought he was talking about something completely different. "Yes! Bags. That's what I call it. But yes, I love that idea!"

And I take that as my green light. He's got a charity, he's got an event, and he's got the passion.

As soon as this ball is over, I've got work to do.

I'll just push my feelings for him aside. That shouldn't be too hard...right?

CHAPTER 6

We grab one more drink before last call, and we dance a little more, and with every step we take on the dance floor, my heart beats a little more strongly for him.

The way his eyes light up when he's passionate about something is beyond endearing. It's pushing my feelings for him into another place that's both dangerous and scary for me considering how adamant he's been that he isn't right for me.

I want him to kiss me.

I want to share a bed with him but for it to be real.

It's too soon, yet I want our engagement to mean something for *us*, not just for the media.

Brandon leaves with his date still plastered to the side of his body, and Luke asks if I'm ready to go not too long after that. He bids his farewells to the people that he knows, and before we slide into the town car waiting for us out in front, I tell him I need to use the restroom. He does, too, and tells me we'll meet in the lobby when we're each done.

I'm riding the high of the night with Luke combined with my ridiculously good idea for a charity event when I'm blindsided in the ladies' room.

I'm washing my hands when the woman at the sink beside me says, "No ring on that third finger."

Is she talking to me?

She's right. I don't have a ring on my finger...even though I'm *engaged*.

"Pardon me?" I say politely. I glance up at the mirror to get a look at her, and she's absolutely gorgeous. Stunning blue eyes and wavy dark hair that cascades down to the middle of her back. Her skin glows and her dress looks like it was made to fit her petite frame. I'm immediately intimidated by her just from the way she's narrowing her eyes at me. She has that resting bitch face thing going on even though she's smiling at me. Is that smiling bitch face?

I grab a paper towel to dry my hands, and she does the same. "I said you're not wearing a ring. Aren't you engaged to Luke Dalton?"

I'm confused. Who is this woman and how does she know who I am? "Yes, we're engaged," I say.

"So why aren't you wearing a ring?" she presses.

"We haven't had time to pick one out." The lie rolls smoothly out of my mouth and I just want to get out of this bathroom and get back to Luke, who's waiting for me in the hallway. I toss my paper towel in the trash, and this woman is right behind me every step of the way, her paper towel going in right on top of mine.

I don't like fielding questions alone. When we're together, at least we can make sure we're telling the same stories.

"When did you get engaged?" she asks, and I'm still walking toward the door to exit this damn bathroom and it must be the biggest bathroom in the history of bathrooms because it feels like this is taking forever.

"A few days ago." I'm about to rush out of there, but then I realize that makes me look like I have something to hide.

"How long have you been together?"

You have a lot of questions for someone who hasn't introduced herself.

I wish I had the guts to say something like that...but I don't. I'm intimidated by this woman, and Luke didn't train me on how to handle rabid fans or whoever this is. I'm a big girl, though. I can handle this.

"We've known each other a while but the timing was never right." I lift a shoulder. "And then it was, and we grabbed our chance."

"Luke said he would never get married again. How did you manage to tie him down?"

My brows dip, and I finally open the door. "I'm sorry, but who are you?"

Luke is standing just down the hallway, and his eyes move toward the two of us.

When he spots the woman beside me, his eyes widen and then he looks just plain angry.

I look over at the woman again, and she flashes me a smirk as we reach Luke.

"Savannah," he says, and the word comes out with venom.

My heart races as I finally realize who she is.

The ex-wife.

After all the research I did, you'd think I would've come across her picture *somewhere* to recognize her, but Luke did a good job keeping his past hidden. I've been so busy learning about wide receivers that I haven't had time to really get into Luke's personal history.

But this is the reporter.

She was digging at me for a story back there in the bathroom.

What a bitch.

"Luke," she says back, entirely too sweetly.

"It's my extreme displeasure to introduce you to my ex-wife, Savannah Buck," he says to me.

"Maybe in a few months when this is all over, we can start an ex-wives club," she says, circling her finger between Luke and me.

"Get the fuck outta here," Luke mutters, and it's clear they did not part amicably. "Why'd you print that lie the other day?"

She raises a perfectly manicured brow. "The *lie*? Excuse me, Mr. Dalton, but I only tell the truth."

He laughs, a hearty and fake laugh filled with malice that I've never heard from him before. "You print whatever's convenient for you that also manages to fuck with my reputation."

Savannah's hand flies to her chest in an act like she's deeply offended. She makes a noise of disbelief, but I don't buy her act for a second. Neither does Luke.

"So if you only print the truth, where's your proof that Michelle is really carrying my child?"

"Big difference in what you're asking there, Captain." Her eyes twinkle like she's enjoying this banter, but Luke looks like he's about to pop a blood vessel in his forehead.

"What, you mean a story versus a story with evidence?" he shoots back, and it's clear he's flustered by this entire conversation while she maintains her cool, and I fucking hate her in that moment. I hate what she's doing to Luke. I hate that she's getting under his skin. I hate that she can stand there and do that to him with such calm confidence.

"You didn't ask for evidence. You asked why I printed a lie, and I didn't. A woman came to me with her claims, and nowhere in the article does it say that there's evidence she's carrying your child. That's why we use words like *alleged*. I know it's hard for your overly concussed brain to grasp, so I'll break it down for you. Lady said she's knocked up with your kid and you're marrying some side chick you've known four seconds."

"Oh fuck you, Savannah," he spits, rolling his eyes. "Come on, Ellie. Let's go home."

She holds up her hands innocently. "Bye bye," she says, and then she winks at Luke as she starts to walk away. "Looking forward to your check, my sweet benefactor." She tosses that final line over her shoulder.

Luke exhales heavily as we head toward the exit. "So that's another reason I didn't want to come tonight, you know, just in case you were wondering."

"Why did she call you her benefactor?" It's a stupid question but apparently the only thing I can think of to say.

"Alimony, although not as much as she'd like and certainly not as much as I'd have to pay if we'd have gotten married now versus seven years ago."

"How long were you married?"

"About a year. I was young and stupid and thought she was hot. Hot does not equal marriage material."

Sage advice indeed. It would probably do me well to remember that.

"Why didn't you contact her boss and demand a retraction?" I ask.

"It's sensationalism. It's unethical, but it's not illegal. She prints her little stories at the expense of accuracy, and unless there's libel or slander involved, it's not illegal."

"Isn't it libel if that baby Michelle is carrying isn't yours?"

He lifts a shoulder and twists his lips a little wistfully. "There's more to it than that. They're both backing me into a corner, and I don't have a choice but to sit back and take it."

The car is waiting for us when we get out front, and it feels very much like the end of that conversation as we slide into the back of the car...but I want to know *why* he doesn't feel like he has a choice.

We're well on our way back to Luke's place, silence blanketing us as he seems like he's deep in thought while I'm not sure what my role is. Should I try to distract him? Let him think it out? Talk? I go with lighthearted small talk. "Did you have fun?"

He shrugs and glances over at me. "As much fun as I always do at these things. Capping the night with my ex-wife wasn't the ideal way to end it."

"Then let's pretend that didn't happen. We can find our own way to cap the night." I wink at him. "At least you had a hot date." Okay, maybe I'm a *tad* tipsy after all the wine.

He chuckles and moves his gaze to the window. "That I did," he says, and it's under his breath so I almost miss it.

But I don't, and I think back to when he called me *Sexy Ellie* when he thought I was asleep.

"So tomorrow I'll look into what it takes to start a charity and how to make it happen," I say, mostly to change the subject and a little because I don't think he realizes I heard what he just said. But honestly...I don't even have a clue as to where to start my research. I don't even know what I don't know.

"I can put you in touch with the charitable contributions department at the Aces to see if they have any guidance," he says almost as if he's reading my mind.

"That would be amazing," I gush.

"Erin's great," he says. "She helped Brandon get his charity off the ground."

"What's his charity?" I ask.

"Fostering Fletch. He raises money that goes to help foster kids," he says. "He can be kind of a douchebag when it comes to women, but deep down he's a pretty good guy."

We pull into Luke's neighborhood.

"How did my brother end up across the street from you?" I ask.

He chuckles. "I had the receivers over one night for beer and poker, and he saw the sign in the yard across the street. We got to talking, laughed about how fun it would be, and he made a lowball offer the next day. They accepted, and the rest is history."

"Do you like Vegas?" I ask.

He nods. "I've been here nearly a decade now. It's home."

"Where'd you grow up?" I ask as we pull into the driveway.

"Michigan. I was recruited by Wisconsin and drafted right out of college by the Aces."

"Lucky Luke," I say.

"My grandfather used to call me that." He chuckles. "Hence the Lucky Charms. But honestly it was luck combined with a little hard work." He opens the door and runs around the car to my side to help me out. He bids goodnight to the driver, and then we walk together up to the front door.

We stand there on the porch for a beat. He watches the driver as he backs out of the driveway, and he hasn't moved to open the door yet.

The light breeze in the night air makes me shiver.

My eyes meet his, and he takes a step toward me. He's close enough for me to feel his heat.

"This is the part of the night where I'd usually kiss my date goodnight," he says softly.

I look up at him as nerves rattle around in my chest.

We've kissed before.

I mean, we've had *sex*, so of course we've kissed too.

I think back to that first kiss in the lounge chair by the pool at the Cosmopolitan, and another shiver runs through me. This one isn't from the chill in the evening air, though.

He reaches beneath my hair to cup my neck, his fingers curling around me as the heat in his eyes turns to an inferno.

He moves a centimeter closer, and my heart races as my knees start to shake.

I want this.

God, do I want him to kiss me.

He moves in even a little closer, his big hand warm on my skin.

That fresh scent of his plows into me.

Kiss me, kiss me, kiss me, I chant in my own head.

And just when I close my eyes to wait for his lips to meet mine, he sighs and pulls away.

He unlocks the front door, and I follow him into the kitchen. He loosens the knot in his tie and unbuttons the first button of his collar, revealing a delicious peek of skin.

I want to lick it. I want to lick *him*. Everywhere.

I want that kiss we missed out on...but I'm afraid the spell has been broken. Whatever drove him to nearly kiss me appears to have evaporated, and I can't recreate the quiet peace that nearly brought us there.

"I'm uh..." he begins. "I'm sorry. I realize I'm sending confusing signals, and I think it's because, well, I'm confused. I like you, Ellie. A lot." He clears his throat as he looks away, and I wish I could get inside his mind and figure out what he's thinking.

"I like you, too." My brows dip down.

He blows out a breath. "This is all just so complicated."

"What is?" I ask.

"I feel like I keep doing all the wrong things. What happens when this is all over?"

"My brother is your best friend. If we fake this engagement for another day or another year, it doesn't matter. He'll still be in your life, which means maybe it's okay for me to be, too."

He nods. "What if I push you away and you hate me?"

"Come on, Luke," I say a little more loudly than may be completely necessary. "You're grasping at straws here. You're finding ways to sabotage our arrangement before it even gets off the ground."

"That's not what I'm doing," he counters. "I'm just being realistic. I'm analyzing. I'm looking at it from all the different angles and perspectives." Just like he does when he studies film.

Looks like I'm not the only one who overanalyzes things.

"What are you so scared of?" I ask.

He doesn't answer, but I think I already know. He hasn't healed from his past relationships. His ex-wife and his ex-girlfriend were manipulative. They scarred him, and now he's scared to get into something with another manipulator, so he's written off relationships.

He wants to focus on his career, and that's an awfully big hurdle for someone like me to overcome...especially when he's so damn stubborn.

"Look, I won't lead you on," he says. He presses his palms to the counter, his elbows straight as he hangs his head down a bit, his eyes focused between his hands. "I like you, and you like me, but I can't give you the kind of future you want."

"You don't know that," I say softly...hopefully. And for the tiniest flicker of a second, I think about a friends with benefits sort of situation. Whatever he decides next, we're faking this thing together for at least the short term. I could get *some* pleasure out of it. But a friends with benefits thing won't work. I'm already falling for him, so adding sex to the mix (again) will only push me there faster.

"Yeah, I do." He presses his lips together a little sadly as he looks up at me. He opens his mouth to say something else, but then he seems to change his mind. "I'm going to go take a shower. Goodnight."

He turns and heads out of the room at that, shattering that tiny ray of hope he gave me when he almost kissed me.

CHAPTER 7

On Monday morning, Luke gives me specific instructions for how to find Erin at the staff offices located inside the practice facility.

"Why are the offices at your practice facility and not at the stadium?" I ask.

"The team doesn't own the stadium," he says.

This is one of those times I don't even know what I don't know. Same with his directions. It's the kind of thing you can't find on your phone's GPS as he explains how to navigate the hallways of the building, and I stare at him like he has two heads.

He glances at his watch. "You want to just go together?"

I nod. His meeting with Calvin starts an hour after my meeting with Erin. "Pretty please?"

He chuckles. "Of course. Let's take two cars, though, because I have a workout planned with Tristan and I don't want you to have to wait around for us to finish."

"Who's Tristan?" I ask.

"The new guy," he says, giving me that look like I know nothing about football again. "Tristan Higgins."

I shrug. "Maybe I could stop by your workout to snap a few pictures for Instagram. Imagine how good it'll make you look. You're extending goodwill toward the new guy, you're confident about your place on the team, you're introducing him to what you do. Plus it would give your fans an insider look of where you work out with the team. They'd love it."

"I'm not doing it to look good. I'm an actual decent guy," he says.

"Yeah," I say softly, thinking of my history of men who really weren't such good guys versus this man who gave the girl he doesn't even know a place to live and a job. "You do seem like you're one of the good ones."

He joins me for my meeting, and there are multiple reasons why it's actually a good thing to have him with me. For one, I *never* would have found Erin's office without him. And for another, I end up looking to him to answer a lot of the questions Erin has. I don't want this to be *my* event. I want it to be his. I want it to be something he can carry with him beyond our time together, however long that might last.

And then I glance over and see how excited he is about this whole charity idea. He can't wait to start raising money to ensure every kid has a fair shot to play sports, that they won't get left behind just because they can't afford the team uniform...that they have a sufficient place to practice and play.

My heart pitter patters.

My stomach flips.

Oh shit.

I knew it was happening.

I could feel it coming, and there was little I could do to stop it.

It's as we sit in this meeting with Erin, excitement lighting his face and passion burning in his eyes that I realize something. That feeling in the pit of my stomach is the low burn of fire as my body tried to warn me. *Stop! Alert! Stop!*

But it's too late. I went and fell for him, and now I'm pretending to be engaged to him while privately he keeps pushing me away.

I've gotten myself into quite the jam.

He transitions into a bundle of nerves as the clock ticks closer and closer to nine-thirty, and then he excuses himself to meet with Calvin while Erin and I work out some more details on our own.

I'm dying to ask him about the meeting once he returns a half hour later, but I don't get the chance, and this isn't the place for him to talk about it, anyway.

Instead, we head to the gym. That fire in my stomach only burns hotter as I take pictures of him working out with the Aces' newest team member.

And it's not until a few hours later as he signals his way onto the highway that I finally ask the question that has been burning in my mind since ten this morning. "How was your meeting with Calvin?"

He clears his throat. "Not great."

"What did he say?"

"He ripped me a new one for knocking up Michelle, and then I had to explain how I'm not the right man for her but I'll be there for her and the baby every step of the way." He's quiet and flat as he speaks, and I can tell the conversation did a number on him even though the workout must've helped him categorize his feelings. "He also reminded me more than once that I'm not the only wide receiver in the league."

"That's awful," I say, reaching over to squeeze his hand.

But I don't get it. Why does Calvin care what Luke does on his own time?

He presses his lips together and keeps his eyes focused forward on the road. "He's right, though. I'm not. I'm easily replaceable, and that's why I need you." He pauses, and my heart races. He *needs* me. Except then he adds, "It's why I need your help with both my image and my brand to make me someone who isn't so easily replaced." His words are a reminder that this is nothing more than a business deal to him...even though it's more than that to me. "He asked me how I'm going to make things right with Michelle. I told him I'm engaged to somebody else now. I hope you're still okay with pretending with me for a while."

I'm still okay with it even if I don't really get why Calvin is so invested.

I just find myself wishing more and more that it wasn't pretend.

CHAPTER 8

After my shower the next morning, I head down to the kitchen with my laptop and grab some coffee before I get to work. I slide onto one of the stools at the counter and I'm munching on a banana when Luke walks in.

"I have something for you," he says.

I glance away from my screen and over at him, my brows dipped down. "What is it?"

"Come with me."

I abandon my laptop and toss the banana peel in the trash. We walk through the house, and he stops at a closed door. It's the office where my boxes have been stacked since the movers dropped them off.

Maybe this is his way of telling me to move my boxes or unpack my shit or just get the hell out because it isn't working for him.

"Open the door," he says softly.

My heart pounds as I do it, and I gasp as I look around.

Gone is the dark wood, replaced with a fresh and completely opposite look. A huge, white desk sits in the middle of the room with a very comfortable looking white chair. Two white chairs sit opposite the desk. Empty white bookshelves line one wall, and floor to ceiling windows give me a gorgeous view into his backyard.

In the center of the room is a fluffy purple rug.

The desk is filled with office accessories.

They're all glittery purple.

A large purple couch sits on the wall across the room from the desk, a place where I can relax and create.

Hanging on the walls I see all sorts of artwork with phrases like *hustle* and *lady boss* and *grind* in glitter. Another one says *work work work,* and another says *I'm not bossy* with its twin photo hanging next to it that reads *I'm the boss.*

It's all purple and white with silver sparkles, and the boxes that were stacked along the wall are gone.

"This is for *me?*" I ask.

Tears fill my eyes as I look at Luke, who looks proud of himself. He nods with that lady killer grin of his.

I move toward the fluffy purple rug and spin in a circle. The fabric is soft on my feet. "When did you do all this?"

"I've been at it a while. Everything was delivered while we were at the ball and I've worked on it the last couple days with Debbie's help."

"But you asked me my favorite color the other day..." I trail off.

He chuckles. "Like I didn't already know. Ellie, your phone is purple. So is your suitcase and most of your clothes."

"And all the glitter?"

"I don't think you've gone a single day without wearing something that sparkles, whether it's your watch band or your shirt or your bright smile."

I melt into a pile of lust for him as my knees feel a little weak. "You noticed all that?"

One side of his mouth lifts. "Of course I did," he says softly.

I can't help when I automatically move toward him and toss my arms around his neck. I want to kiss him. Every urge inside me is telling me to kiss him.

And I do...but I go for his cheek, and then I untangle myself from him. I walk over to the desk and open one of the drawers.

A bunch of my bullet journal stuff is in there, all organized neatly. "Thank you. This is incredible."

"I figured if you're going to be here working for me, you deserve to have your own space. Even if it's just temporary. I'm sure you love the kitchen counter, but that ergonomic chair will be a little easier on your back than the barstool."

"This is the nicest thing anyone has ever done for me," I say softly.

We stare at each other as heat passes between us.

He's agile and athletic, his black shirt clinging to his broad chest and his charcoal shorts making his legs look lean and muscled. His eyes are on me, and he almost looks a little nervous.

"Can we, uh, talk a second?" he asks, and a dart of anxiety rushes through my chest as I wonder whether the gift of this office is about to be tainted by this conversation.

"Of course," I say, and neither of us moves from where we stand.

"I know we haven't exactly figured out the logistics of our fake engagement, but between running into Savannah at the ball and my conversation with Calvin...I feel like we need to push forward with this idea if you're still okay with it."

"Push forward with what?" I ask. I'm confused as to what he's getting at. We've already agreed to faking this, so it's like he's a step behind me and he can't quite catch up.

"I don't even know how to ask this, or what the hell I'm doing, and your brother is going to fucking murder me...but I mean an actual fake marriage." He shakes his head and looks out the window. "I can't believe I'm even suggesting it."

My brows dip. "I thought you were against the idea. What changed your mind?"

He sighs. "Getting reamed by my boss got me thinking, and I'm not sure I see any other solution. And, obviously, I'd make sure you walk away with a healthy payday."

"Why does your boss care so much about your private life?"

He looks at me in confusion for a beat like it's a silly question, but then a light seems to dawn in his eyes. "Oh, you don't know." He clears his throat. "Michelle's last name is Bennett. She's Calvin's daughter."

My eyes widen. "She's his *daughter*?"

Well, I guess that explains Calvin's investment in this whole thing. Suddenly everything falls into place.

Now I understand why he feels backed into a corner...and why he isn't demanding a paternity test just yet. He can't make a big public stink about this or he risks pissing off the team owner in a contract year. It makes much more sense for him to just lie low and let the media frenzy blow over.

Man, he really is stuck between a rock and a hard place.

"I think an actual marriage might be the only way to shut Savannah up and keep Michelle from trying to squeeze the life out of me while also getting Calvin to understand that even though I'll be there for both her and the baby, marriage isn't in the cards for Michelle and me."

"But what if it doesn't?" I ask, and I'm not sure why, exactly, my dumb ass is trying to talk him *out* of this idea where I get to marry a hot football player who happens to be my brother's best friend and also the guy who I have a raging, massive crush on.

He blinks in surprise. "What if it doesn't...what?"

I lean my ass on the edge of my brand-new desk. "What if it doesn't shut Savannah up? What if it doesn't keep Michelle off your back? What if it doesn't prove anything to Calvin? We haven't given it much of an effort, but it doesn't seem like being *engaged* has worked. Why do you think marriage will?

Long **GAME**

Maybe I need to get knocked up, too." I say that last part as a joke, but Luke pauses and raises his brows like he's considering the idea. My heart falls into my stomach. "Oh Jesus. I'm kidding, Luke."

He laughs. "Gotcha."

"Dude." I walk across the few steps between us and smack his shoulder. "Not cool." I take a second to look out the window and regroup. I can't stare at Luke's hot face and make a rational decision.

I haven't thought this through.

It's stupid. Everyone would tell me that.

And yet...it feels somehow like the right thing to do. He offered me a place to stay before he knew a damn thing about me, and so I'm offering him this as a way to help him out of his own mess. Plus, you know, that whole *healthy payday* thing. It would give me the chance to find my own place and maybe even start my own PR firm.

I like him a little more every second I spend with him. It's not like this is *all* bad.

And that's why I'm leaning toward a yes here. It's my job to clean up his image. To make him indispensable to the Aces. To prove to the world that he's as amazing as I think he is. And if I need to be his wife to do that...then it's sort of part of my job description, isn't it? And as his wife, I don't think it's necessarily outside my wifely duties to demand a paternity test from his pregnant ex since he doesn't feel like he can.

God, I'm riding a fine line here. I really need to be more careful about what I wish for.

I'm going with my heart, clearly not my brain, as I speak my next words. "I don't know. It isn't the *worst* idea in the world, is it? If you really think a fake marriage is going to help you, I'm still in."

"Maybe we should leave it up to fate," he muses.

I raise a brow. "Fate?"

He shrugs. "Let's hit the casino tonight."

"That's not fate," I point out. "That's a gamble. I prefer to be in charge of my own life decisions."

He laughs. "We're in Vegas, baby. Let's gamble."

I don't like the idea of this, but I'm starting to find that when Luke asks, I agree. And so, after dinner, we head to the Strip.

He navigates to the valet parking of Caesar's Palace, and he grabs my hand. A tingle buzzes around my chest and my stomach does a little flip. I don't know if he does it because we're in public or if he does it because he wants to hold my hand. I hope it's the latter, but I have a sinking feeling he's just trying to show off our relationship should he be recognized by anyone.

We head inside and walk through the expansive casino toward a bar. He glances at me. "Want anything?"

I'm not sure if this is a *get wasted* kind of visit to the bar or more of a *have one and we'll head home* kind of visit, but I order a glass of white wine and he opts for a whiskey sour.

He pays, and we take our drinks toward a room marked *High Limit*. I may be new to Vegas, but I'm pretty sure they're not talking about alcohol.

The room is empty except for one older couple playing a slot machine in the corner. He pulls out his wallet, grabs a hundred dollar bill, and sits at a poker machine. I sit in the open chair next to him.

"You go first," he says. "If we double our money or more, we get married."

I stare at him for a beat.

He's serious.

And I'm not going to be the one to back down.

Long **GAME**

I push the button to deal the cards, my heart thumping so loudly in my chest that I'm afraid he'll hear it. It's five card draw, so I get five cards, I can discard as many as I want, and I'm dealt enough to make it five again. If I get a pair or higher, I win…or, at least I don't lose.

I get a two, a four, a six, an eight, and nine. All shit cards. I press the button to get all new cards, and I get about the same shit I had on the first hand.

He tries next, and it's the same shit, different hand. My heart is still thumping, but the initial nerves over this whole idea are starting to dissipate as I realize there's no way in hell we're going to win.

He nods for me to go, and I lose. Zero cards go together to attempt to make any sort of hand.

He goes again, and he loses.

We go back and forth, and when we get down to our last ten dollars, he says, "Let's push the button together."

I nod, lean in so close I can smell him, and set my finger on the button. He places his on top of mine and pushes down.

The cards seem to flip in slow motion.

King of hearts.

Ten of hearts.

Queen of hearts.

Ace of hearts.

And a fucking four of spades.

He looks at me with wide eyes, and I'm sure my gaze back mirrors his.

If we snag a jack of hearts, that's a royal flush, and that's the top jackpot payout on this machine—twenty-five thousand dollars.

That's more than *doubling* our money.

He saves the ten, queen, king, and ace, and then I set my finger on the button.

He presses my finger.

I squeeze my eyes shut because I can't look. I'm too damn nervous.

"Holy fuck," he murmurs close to my ear, and that's when I know.

My eyes pop open. "Oh my God!" I squeal when I spot the jack of hearts in the place where that four was sitting before. The machine starts going crazy, and the jackpot song plays as a big, blue stripe across the center of the screen screams, "JACKPOT! Hand pay required."

We're both in shock. We stare at the screen, and then we look at each other, and then we look back at the screen, and holy shit we let fate decide and fate is absolutely pushing us together—for this fake marriage, at least. He leans in and presses a soft kiss to my lips, and I want to hold on for more. I want to straddle his lap and hump him right here as we celebrate our big win, but it's a quick celebratory kiss because we just won twenty-five thousand dollars in a public place.

"I guess we've got our wedding budget," he says, and I burst into giggles.

CHAPTER 9

We're both a little drunk by the time the Uber drops us back in Luke's driveway, and when we get into the kitchen, I drop my purse on the counter and kick off my shoes.

So we're really doing this.

I have hundreds of questions, but I have no idea where to even start and all the celebratory wine I had mixed with coming down off the thrill of winning is making me sleepy. We can deal with the questions in the morning.

To my surprise, though, Luke steps closer to me and grabs my hand. He links his fingers through mine. "Thanks for a fun night, Ellie. You're making me see that not all women are evil."

I laugh, but he doesn't.

"I'm serious." He pulls our joined hands up and presses a feather light kiss to my knuckles.

My knees go weak.

"I'm not like them," I whisper. "I won't manipulate you. I won't hurt you. I'll just be here for you. However you need me to be."

He leans a little closer. "You're definitely going to hurt me." His warm whiskey breath mixes with his Luke scent so close to me, and it overwhelms my senses.

"Why do you think that?" I ask, genuinely curious as I wonder whether whiskey is some sort of truth serum or if it's just a horndog pill and he's coming onto me.

"You already have." He leans even closer, and his nose brushes mine. I think he's going to kiss me, but I'm not sure.

My chest buzzes with excitement, and my legs nearly give out as my hands start to tremble. My body responds even though my brain is trying to do the right thing. I don't even know what the right thing is at this point. We just let a fucking poker machine decide we're getting married.

And I want him.

God, do I want him.

My mind races back to our night together. Snippets here and there—his hand on my ass as he pounded into me from behind. A stolen kiss on a lounge chair by the pool.

"How?" I ask, my breath a whisper just inches from his mouth.

"By being you. By being everything I want but nothing I can have." His lips brush mine, and everything inside me lights with fire as rockets explode in my chest.

"But you *can* have me, Luke," I argue softly against his lips.

He shakes his head as if my words sober him for a beat. "No," he says. "I can't. I'll only hurt you in the end. It's what I do. My past relationships that ended...there were two people involved, and I'm not innocent. You're too good for that." He brushes his lips across mine again. "You're too goddamn good for me." He kisses me just for a second where it's more than a brush of lip on lip, it's a tender press of his mouth to mine, but then he pulls back from me. He backs up a step.

"Goodnight," he says softly, and then he strides out of the room.

I'm not sure where he goes, but I give him some time in case he went upstairs to the bedroom we're sharing.

When I finally go up to bed, though, he's not in there. My heart drops with disappointment.

He must be sleeping in one of the guest rooms, which is probably a good thing considering the amount of alcohol we both had tonight.

Drunk or not, I want another night with him.

I want all the nights, but I'd settle for one.

* * *

I'm in *my office* working on some community outreach for Luke when he knocks on the doorframe.

"You can just walk in," I say a little more testily than I intend to. "It is your house, you know."

"I know," he says. "I just wanted to say I'm sorry about last night."

"Which part?" I ask a little flippantly, my eyes returning to my laptop screen. Does he mean the part where he let a slot machine decide our fate, the part where he kissed me and then bolted, or the part where he said he's no good for me? It appears he has much to apologize for.

"All of it, but mostly for kissing you."

"I'm not." My eyes flick to his. "Anything else?"

He sighs. "Do you still want to do this thing with me?"

"First, don't call it a *thing*, and second, I have no idea why, but sure, why not."

His brows both rise in surprise, like he was sure I was going to back out. "I still don't understand why, either, but if you really are on board, then I'm not going to question it."

I glance up at him, and he seems conflicted where he stands as his gaze falls to the window. "Did you want to win on that machine?" I ask.

His eyes slide over to mine. "I've never lost on it," he says softly.

I'm glad I'm sitting, because my knees would freaking give out if I wasn't.

"So I guess we should make it official." He draws in a shaky breath, and then he shifts as he moves to get down on one knee. He grabs something from his pocket, a little box, and he flips open the lid.

I gasp.

I'm still sitting at my damn desk.

"Ellie Nolan, will you be my wife?" he says.

Of all the scenarios I imagined upon receiving a ring for the first time from the man of my dreams, faking it was never part of the story. Sitting behind a desk while he asked was also not part of the story.

Yet here we are.

I stand up, my demeanor softening, and I walk around the desk to where he kneels.

I smile down at him. "I'd love to," I say, and I'm a little scared at how very much I mean those words.

It's only going to mean bad news for me when it's all over.

He slides the rock onto my hand, and I can't help when I bring it up a little closer to inspect it. It's gorgeous and the diamond is almost heavy it's so big. Way too big.

But beautiful.

And mine.

It's square with smaller diamonds surrounding it set in a platinum band. It must've cost a fortune, and it sparkles in the bright white office where we stand. I already know I'll always look at the spot where Luke kneels and think of this moment.

I just have no idea how I'll *feel* when I look at this spot.

In all those scenarios I imagined for my engagement moment, I also never really thought the guy who just proposed to me would seal the deal with a quick hug and a whispered *thanks*, but that's exactly what happens.

"When are we doing this?" I ask, in part because I'm afraid I'll change my mind if I have too much time to think about it and partly because I'm worried *he* will change his mind. I back up and lean against my desk since my knees are still a little shaky.

He stands as he draws in a breath, and then he collapses on my couch. *My* couch. The one he got for me and put in *my* office. I'm still a little awestruck over that. "Probably before your brother gets back from his honeymoon."

I nod. That only gives us about two and a half weeks. Holy cheese and crackers. "Definitely. And are we having a wedding or is this a City Hall affair?"

"Well..." he says, and then he trails off like he just had an idea.

"What?"

"We're supposed to go to Hawaii in a couple weeks. What if we surprise my family with a wedding while we're there?"

"You'd be okay getting married as a lie in front of your family?" I ask.

"It's not a lie that we're getting married," he points out. "We *are* actually getting married. It's just the whole, you know, barely knowing each other thing that we can leave out of the conversation."

I press my lips together. If he's okay with it, I guess I'm okay with it, too.

"And what'll we tell people is our reason for the rush?" I ask, trying to cover all the angles as I glance down at my ring again.

I can't help it.

"Love." He says the word so simply that I almost believe him.

My eyes flick over to his. "How long will we stay married?"

He lifts a shoulder, and I can't help but think he looks a little sad sitting there on the couch. I have this strange urge again to hug him, and even though I'm going to be his wife, I'm still not sure we're there. "A year? I don't want to tie you up any longer than that but it should give me enough time to deal with all this." He waves a hand through the air.

To deal with all this. That's why we're doing this.

I'm still not exactly sure why I agreed. I have literally nothing else going on when it comes to career, abode, or my love life. Whatever the case, I'm going to be someone's wife in three weeks.

Or less.

Suck on that, Todd.

CHAPTER 10

The feelings I've now identified that I'm having for him are exacerbated further when I show him the selection of tuxedoes he can pick from for our surprise wedding in Hawaii. And it's physically painful as I scroll through wedding dresses as I try to find a good destination option that'll travel well and still be perfect for our day.

I push those feelings down, down, down. Ignoring that I'm falling for him is my only option.

He sets up the cornhole boards in his backyard and challenges me to a tournament, and, never one to back down from a challenge, I agree.

That was my first mistake.

As I may have mentioned, I'm not the most coordinated person on the planet.

He explains the rules to me, positions me next to the board he will toss his beanbags to, and tells me to toss my bag onto the board he will be standing by. He tells me the goal is to try to get my beanbag right into the hole, and I nod him off since I've played this game before and just didn't know it was called *Cornhole*.

And my first toss of my beanbag toward Luke's board hits him right in...well, his beanbag.

He doubles over and grabs his crotch in pain, and I rush the thirty-or-so feet across the yard to check to be sure he's okay. "Oh my God, Luke! I'm so sorry!" I put my arm around his shoulders awkwardly as he moans and falls to the ground, still grasping himself.

"Are you okay?" I yell, and I don't know why I'm yelling except maybe I'm panicking a little that I actually hurt him.

He chuckles and sits up, his hands not moving from covering his crotch, and dammit I can't pretend like I don't wish those were my hands there. "I'm being a *little* dramatic, but damn, girl, you've got quite an arm on you."

I smack him in the arm, and he moves one hand to rub that spot. "You had me really worried about you!"

"Sorry. But seriously, where the hell did you learn to throw like that?"

I lift a shoulder then sit on the grass beside him. "The force or the aim?"

He laughs. "I'm talking about the force since the aim could use a little work."

I shrug. "From Josh? I mean clearly I have no idea of my own strength since I really thought that would sail right into the hole."

"Maybe we need a little more practice before the event," he says.

"Speaking of which, when do you want to actually hold the event?"

He glances over at me. "Before the season starts if we can. If not, we'll need to wait until it's over."

"Preliminary research tells me we can have the event without the proper paperwork on hand so long as we disclose our tax status to donors ahead of time." I cross my legs crisscross-applesauce and pick at a blade of grass.

He finally lets go of his crotch, and he stretches his legs out in front of him. "So we could have it next week if we wanted."

"Theoretically, yes. But bear in mind the woman planning it is also planning a wedding and managing your public relations and doesn't think she could handle the stress of executing a charity event in a week."

He laughs. "What the fuck am I paying you for?"

It's a clear joke, and I giggle. "When do you report back for training camp?"

"End of July," he says.

"And what's that like? Could we hold it then?"

He gives me a look like I'm insane. "Uh, no."

"Why not?"

"It's grueling. Harder than the actual season. It's where we show what we're made of. We arrive at six in the morning and don't get home until ten or eleven most nights. I get three, maybe four days off for the entire month of August. There just wouldn't be time."

"Then we do it before training camp," I say. "Year one can be a trial run with just the people in your circle, and next year we can plan for a huge blowout."

He catches his bottom lip between his teeth, and God I wish I could catch that lip between *my* teeth, and then he nods. "Okay. Let's do it."

I grab the calendar, we pick a date that falls the weekend before training camp begins…and then I get to work.

* * *

"A little closer," I say, and his body is nearly pressed against mine.

Oh yeah, baby. Right there.

I try not to sigh as I click the remote in my hand to snap a photo of the two of us. My phone is on a tripod a few feet away from us. The palm trees surrounding his pool are behind us, with the mountains as a backdrop beyond those, and the sun at the perfect angle as it starts to set. We're smiling in the background of this photo as I hold my ring up to the camera after a fresh manicure this morning.

"Now one of us kissing," I say, and I turn toward him.

Any excuse to get those lips back on mine.

This is for my job, though. I need to stir up a little publicity, to show that he's in love with me, to make him look like he's heading toward his happily ever after and that he really is engaged to silence people like Savannah. Posting a ring pic seems like a good start.

He brushes his lips with mine, and I get so lost in the feel of his mouth on mine again that I nearly forget to click the remote.

He stops it first, and I turn away and walk toward my phone to check our work. I pretend like I'm unaffected by his kiss...but I'm not.

I'm *totally* affected by it.

I wish he felt the same. I wish I could understand why he was so adamant this can't work between us because the more time I spend with him, the more convinced I become that it *would* work.

I clicked the button three times in the short window I had, and I love all three options. There's no way to choose the best one. Studying those three pictures later as I try to decide which one to post will definitely not be the worst part of my day.

Except maybe it will. I'm only hurting myself here. I have the option of walking away, but when I think about that, my stomach seems to turn over with knots. Maybe that's an option because that's *always* an option, but it's not one I'm willing to take. Now that I've met Luke Dalton, I want to be a part of his life.

Even if I have to get hurt in the process. Just being a player in this game will have to be enough for me. Well, that mixed with the hope that someday he'll feel the same way I do.

Time seems to pass in the blink of an eye between working on getting a charity off the ground, planning a wedding, and managing a celebrity's public relations—a celebrity who, by the way, is in the spotlight because of this baby news, and suddenly it's the night before we leave for Hawaii.

I've been shopping for days, and I've managed to get all the outfits I need for a wedding plus fun in the sun…and even a *just-in-case* negligee should the opportunity present itself on our wedding night. Or any other night of our trip.

We met with the lawyer and the paperwork has been signed. We even got our marriage license, so we'll be legal once the ceremony is performed. It all came together incredibly quickly, and now it's time to pack.

The wedding gown is in a garment bag along with a few other dresses I decided to bring along, and it's hanging unzipped on my side of the closet when Luke walks in.

I jump up from where I'm kneeling on the floor as I survey my clothes, and I zip the bag shut.

He laughs. "I don't think the whole thing about it being bad luck to see the dress before the wedding applies when it's fake."

I purse my lips. "While that may be true, I don't want to tempt fate."

"Suit yourself," he says. He grabs a suitcase down from the top shelf and starts tossing clothes into it. While I have an outfit for each day laid out on the closet floor beside my suitcase, he's literally just tossing in a handful of shirts, a couple pairs of shorts, some swim trunks, and jeans.

"Don't forget your wedding tux," I remind him, and he nods toward a garment bag similar to mine hanging on his side of the closet. I slide back down to my knees in front of my clothes. I stack three outfits I'm definitely taking with and set them gently into my suitcase.

"Got it." He's quiet a beat while he organizes the clothes he tossed into his luggage, and then he asks, "Are you ready for all this?"

I turn around and find that he's sitting on the floor, watching me as I sort my clothes. He's leaning against the shelving unit on his side.

I sit back and lean on my own shelves directly across from him. We're maybe eight feet apart, and it feels too far. "Ready for what? Being Luke Dalton's wife?" I tease with a smile.

He lifts a shoulder and doesn't crack a smile like I expect him to. "Meeting my family. Getting married. The media frenzy that'll surely follow."

My smile fades. "What's your family like?" I've gotten snippets here and there, but I don't really know Luke all that well...and yet I've agreed to marry him. "I'm at a slight disadvantage here considering you know my family pretty well."

He shoots me a sad smile that's a little hollow, a rare glimpse into what he's thinking. "Sometimes I wish I was born into a family more like yours."

My brows dip. "You do?"

"Yeah." His tone is a little wistful. "We're not close. I wish I had the kind of dynamic you and Josh share."

"Didn't you say Kaylee texts you a few times a week?" I ask, recalling one of the few times he's talked about his family.

"Yeah, but she's a decade younger than me. She's in college and I've been in my career for almost ten years. She wasn't even old enough to go to a bar and have a drink with me until a couple months ago, and I've been married and divorced and now I'm getting married again." He blows out a breath and shakes his head. "We're just at very different stages of life."

"That doesn't mean you can't be close," I point out.

"I know," he concedes softly. He picks at the plush carpet, and it strikes me that it's kind of odd to be having such a deep conversation with him in his closet. "I just don't put in the effort. It's easier to keep myself closed off."

"Even from them?" I ask immediately even as I realize that while it's in his nature to keep himself closed off, he's actually opening up to me right now. The thought sends a buzz through my chest.

"Especially from them. Kaylee and my mom are close. Jack and my dad are close. Kaylee would run to my mom with any tidbit about me, my mom would tell my dad, and it would get back to Jack. It's stupid family politics bullshit. I can't be myself around them. I have to put on an act."

"That's awful. I'm so sorry," I say, and I mean it. I can't imagine having a relationship like that with Josh. He's my best friend, and he married my best friend, and I love them both so much. I'm so grateful I have them in my life.

But every family is different, and sometimes I wonder what my relationship with Josh would be like if there was another sibling in the picture. Would all three of us be close? Or would one of us always feel left out? Luke seems to feel left out of his own family even though he hasn't actually admitted that.

"Why don't you want things getting back to Jack?" I ask.

"Jack is..." he trails off as he searches for the right words. "He's complicated. He's the kind of guy who always gets his way, and I've been burned more than once because of that."

I'm curious to know more about that, but I don't want to interrupt when he's in the middle of letting me in. I haven't even met Jack yet and I already don't like him just based on the few things Luke has said. I just hope I can keep my feelings to myself when we do meet in a few days.

"So what's a typical Dalton family vacation like? What can I expect?"

He shrugs. "We usually meet for dinner the first night, and then it sort of depends. Since this was Kaylee's choice, she gets to pick a few family outings and the rest is usually free time. Based on how well I know my sister, I'd guess we'll be doing things like sunset dinner cruises and whatever typical tourist traps we can find."

I'm starting to get a little nervous about meeting his family…and what this trip has in store for us.

CHAPTER 11

The car pulls up in front of our hotel, and I can see straight through the open lobby and out to the beach. The white marble floors paired with massive arches, gorgeous greenery, and a ginormous fountain right in the middle of the lobby tell me this hotel is a paradise oasis...and it's mine to enjoy for the next ten days. You know, with the guy I have a huge crush on that I'm actually going to marry while I'm here—the guy who doesn't return my feelings even though we shared that one spectacularly hot night.

I sigh as that old cliché of a warning haunts my thoughts. *Be careful what you wish for.* I wished for a one-night stand. Sure, that's what I got...but somehow I also got a roommate, a boss, and a fiancé. Funny how that worked out.

And in a couple days, I'll be meeting my future in-laws. I'll have to put on an act like the two of us are so in love when this is nothing more than a publicity stunt. My chest aches at the thought.

We're promptly lei-ed with fresh orchids when we get out of the car, and we check in and head to our room— a corner wraparound suite, incidentally, but this one has a separate bedroom unlike the one in Vegas. I take a quick glance out the windows at our view of the beach as I fight off the memories of my hands pressed up against the glass while he took me from behind.

The view is different, but the urges are the same. I wanted him in that hotel room in Vegas when he was nothing more than a stranger, and I want him even more now that I've had a few weeks to get to know him.

I'm falling for him.

Actually, that's not true. It's even worse. I've *fallen* for him.

I turn from the windows and bump right into Luke.

"Oof," I mutter, and he grabs onto my biceps to steady me. "Sorry. I didn't know you were right behind me."

I glance up at him, and our eyes lock. His twinkle down at me as he lets off a soft chuckle. "Nice view," he says, his eyes still on me.

A beat of heated silence passes between us, and is it thick with sexual tension or is that totally just my imagination?

He finally flicks his eyes to the window, and I step out of his grasp because I have to. I was seconds from reaching my hand around his neck and pulling him to me. Seconds from stripping naked and pressing my hands on the glass and sticking my ass out so he could take me again.

Okay, so it's getting warm in here. I step toward the air conditioner and set it cooler, and then I slip my lei over my head and set it on the desk. I check my phone, and then I glance back at Luke, who's staring out over the water deep in thought.

"What's on your mind?" I ask softly.

My voice seems to startle him from his thoughts. He turns from the window back toward me. He exhales, and he offers a small smile. "Nothing. What time's our meeting with the wedding coordinator?"

I glance at the clock. "We've got an hour."

"Are you hungry?" he asks.

I lift a shoulder. "Not really." I do have a wedding dress to fit into in just a couple days, after all.

"Me neither," he mutters. "Want to explore the hotel?"

I nod, and we set off on a walk of the grounds. This particular resort was voted the best luxury accommodations in Maui, and it offers six restaurants, four bars, and three pools. It sits directly on Polo Beach, and we walk around the gorgeous, plush hotel before we slip off our shoes to walk on the sand. People sunbathe all around us as it's a little before three in the afternoon, and soon they'll head inside to shower and get ready for a romantic night out.

I want to reach for his hand because there's something about a beach that's *always* romantic to me…but this is just pretend. I can grab his hand in a few days when it's for the benefit of his family watching us. While there's always the chance there may be paparazzi around somewhere, right now we're just two people walking side-by-side down the beach.

We walk toward the ocean and dip our feet in. The water is warmer than I was expecting, but I've learned lately that my expectations rarely meet reality.

We rinse our feet and head back inside to the lobby, where Alana, our wedding planner, told us to meet her.

"Luke and Ellie?" a woman with long dark hair wearing a flower-patterned dress asks. "I'm Alana," she says when we both glance up at her, and I can't help but languish in the sound of our two names side by side.

Ellie Dalton.

If I had a notebook and a hot pink gel pen and I was ten years younger, I'd be doodling my new name and hearts all over the page.

"How'd you know it was us?" Luke asks.

"You have that soon-to-be-wed glow," she says warmly, and while her sentiment is meant to be sweet, it just makes me feel sad.

Luke laughs, and I offer a smile.

"Let's start with where your ceremony will take place," she says, and we make small talk with her as we follow her out to the beach we just walked in from. She shows us the general area and explains how it'll be set up and how we'll have privacy for our ceremony.

"The bride will stand here," she says, and she stands in place and motions for me to come over because I'm the *bride*.

It's all more than a little surreal. I was dating someone else what feels like five minutes ago and suddenly I'm marrying this guy I've known four minutes. What the hell am I doing?

"The groom will go here," Alana says, and Luke moves into place beside me.

"Take her hands in yours, Luke," she instructs, and he does.

"Manny will be presiding over your vows, and he'll stand here where I am," she says. "Your only job will be to hold one another's hands and look into each other's eyes as you listen to his words, repeat after him for your vows, and then you'll be husband and wife."

Luke's eyes are on mine as she speaks, and my heart pitter-patters. He's only doing it because she's telling us to, but a girl can still wish there was more to it, right?

Alana shows us the restaurant where we'll have our rehearsal dinner and another restaurant where we'll have our reception with Luke's family there to celebrate our new titles as husband and wife. She takes us back to her office, where we review all the details, and then we're done, and while I should be elated that this is going down in just a couple days, instead I feel...hollow.

My family isn't here to celebrate.

I don't even have any friends here. The only people who will witness our vows are people he doesn't really even want at his wedding.

"Are you hungry now?" Luke asks as we stand in the hallway and I debate whether I should tell him my thoughts. "The place where our reception is going to be looked pretty good."

"That's fine," I say, and we head in that direction.

The hostess seats us in a quiet corner booth, and once we've both had a chance to look over the menu and placed our drink orders, he glances across the table at me. "You've been quiet since Alana told us where to stand for our wedding. Are you okay?"

I lift a shoulder and glance away, and then I pick up my wineglass to have something to do with my mouth rather than answering.

"If you're having second thoughts, it's okay to back out," he says quietly. "I know we signed the paperwork, but we don't *have* to do this."

I raise a brow. "Are *you* having second thoughts?" I ask.

"Second…third…fourth." His voice is low as he speaks candidly. "I haven't thought this was a great idea from the start, but I don't know how else to get Michelle and Savannah to back down and also appease Calvin to show him and the world I'm not some horny playboy who fucked around on his little girl."

I chuckle at his assessment but it's not really all that funny. "It just feels weird that no one's here from my family," I admit. "Won't that look kind of strange?"

He shakes his head. "We take this family trip every year and we're doing it as a surprise. Can't we just spin it that we wanted to keep it secret so it was private for the two of us?"

"We can spin it however we want. I guess that's the direction I was planning to go anyway," I say, but his words are just another reminder that this is all for show.

A beat of quiet passes between us as he takes a sip of his beer, and then he says, "Thank you for all you're doing for me. I just want you to know that you always have an out."

"I know I do," I say softly, and I think back to the contract the lawyer drew up. It protects his assets, obviously, but it also protects me. Luke specifically wanted it that way, and it was just one more thing about him that dropped him decidedly into the *prince* category.

The waiter comes by with some bread, and I keep my hands busy by tearing a piece into shreds. "Have you been to Hawaii before?" I ask, changing the subject.

He nods. "Savannah and I came here on our honeymoon. But not Maui. We went to Oahu."

"What was that like?"

"Beautiful beaches, but a totally different pace than here. Maui seems more...I don't know. Relaxing. We stayed in Honolulu and it just has more of a bustling city vibe even right there on the beach. The shopping, the hustle and bustle...that's Savannah's style."

"What's your vacation style?" I ask.

"I like a mix of adventure and relaxation."

"What sort of adventure?"

He shrugs. "ATVs, snorkeling, scuba diving, ziplines, horseback riding. Any kind of tour where I can learn about the place I'm visiting. What's your vacation style?"

"More the relaxing on the beach side, but I'm always up for an adventure. Not, like, adrenaline junkie stuff like ATVs and ziplines, and certainly not horseback riding, but tours or dinner cruises. I read about a submarine outing here in Maui and there's this black beach I'd love to go check out," I say.

"Why not horseback riding?" he asks.

I narrow my eyes and hold up my hands. "You've already started converting me into a football fan, but I have to put my foot down at horseback riding. I *hate* horses."

He laughs. "Why?"

My cheeks heat. "I fell off one when I was younger. I guess I never got over the fear that he was going to trample me."

His brows dip, and it's a rare serious moment from the usually lighthearted girl I am. He reaches across the table and squeezes my hand. "We don't have to go horseback riding. There are plenty of other excursions we can plan before my family gets here."

My heart twists as he inches his hand away from mine, but I pretend like I don't feel it. "I'm sure excursions will provide some amazing backdrops for thirst traps, too," I say, trying to err on the side of professional since if I don't, I might just reveal how I'm starting to feel about this guy.

He chuckles. "We're on vacation, babe. Let's just have some fun." He sips his beer, and I chug my wine, and goodness gracious I'm in a heap of trouble.

CHAPTER 12

His side of the bed is empty when I wake, and the bedroom of our suite is still dark thanks to the heavy curtains blocking out the sunlight. I brush my teeth and use the restroom and then I head off to find my fiancé.

The main living area of our suite is swathed in sunlight, and I spot Luke out on the balcony sitting in a chair with a cup of coffee as he stares out over the ocean. I snap a picture from inside. It might not be a thirst trap, but it's an awfully gorgeous view as far as I'm concerned.

I grab my own cup of coffee from the little pot he made and join him out on the balcony. "Good morning," I say as I push the slider door closed. I sit in the open chair beside him.

"Morning," he says. His eyes are shaded by sunglasses.

"Sleep good?" I ask.

He shrugs. "Sure. You?"

"Yep." I take a sip of coffee and wonder why things feel a little awkward between us this morning, but then I remember that we hardly know each other and maybe this is just him on vacation in the morning. "You ready for your family to get here?"

He chuckles. "No. Not at all. I'm grateful for the next two days we have of actual vacation before the family political matches begin."

I'm quiet in response to that.

"It'll be nice to see Kaylee," he concedes. "A week is just a long time."

"At least you have me," I say with a big, cheesy grin, and he laughs.

"You're right there. You've sort of slipped right into the slot of my best friend over the last few weeks."

"Same goes for you, Hot Luke." My eyes widen as I call him the nickname I usually reserve for my inner thoughts.

He glances at me but doesn't say anything before returning his gaze to the water. I wish I knew what he was thinking, but I *never* know what he's thinking.

I clear my throat awkwardly. His quiet demeanor and pensiveness are throwing me off this morning. "You wanna grab breakfast or something?" I finally ask.

Rather than answer my question, he poses one of his own. "Why are you marrying me?"

I turn to look at him, but he keeps his gaze focused out on the water.

I'm quiet a beat before I answer. "You're giving me a place to live. You're my boss. You're a good guy, Luke, even though you pretend like you're not. You're my brother's best friend. You're becoming *my* best friend. My job is to help turn your image around, and I'm nothing if not dedicated to my work."

And I'm falling in love with you and I think you're falling for me, too, but you're too scared to admit it so you're pushing me away, but maybe over the next year I can make you see how right we are for each other.

I leave that last part out, obviously.

He presses his lips together and nods. "Thanks."

I'm not sure exactly what he's thanking me for—whether it's my explanation or the fact that I'm going to go through with this marriage—but I say, "You're welcome."

"Do you want to just eat up here?" he asks. "Can't beat the views."

I don't even need to glance out over the water where he's looking. I keep my gaze trained on him instead. "You're certainly right about that," I murmur.

"Pick out what you want from the room service menu and I'll call in an order."

A half hour later, our omelets and bacon are delivered.

"No Lucky Charms?" I ask.

"Not even on the menu." He shakes his head and rolls his eyes. "What kind of second-rate place is this?"

I laugh as we keep our eyes on the water and make small talk. Hot coffee sits in a carafe on the tray, and I tip the bottle of vodka I found in our room over my orange juice.

He holds up his glass, too. "Hook me up, future wife," he says lightly, and I giggle as I pour.

"What do you want to do today?" I ask.

"I was just about to ask you the same," he says. "You first."

"I'd lie on the beach and float in the ocean, or we could go to that black beach we talked about. What about you?" I sip my vodka. That's right. My orange juice is gone, so now it's just straight vodka. I'm on vacation.

"What if we do what you want today and what I want tomorrow?" he asks. He tips some vodka into his empty orange juice glass, too.

"And then we meet your family the next day?" I ask.

"Yeah," he murmurs. "Guess we better do what you want both days."

I laugh. "I'm all for equal opportunity. What's on the agenda for tomorrow?"

"Guess you'll find out tomorrow." He raises a brow in my direction, and I purse my lips. Then I shrug, take another sip of vodka, and head in to take a quick shower while Luke gets our tour booked.

When I emerge, Luke is waiting with a backpack. "Our tour is booked, and it's a full day thing, so we need to get our asses downstairs because our tour guide is already waiting for us."

"That was quick."

He smiles. "They were able to slip us in at the last minute, so we got lucky."

I can't help but wonder if we got lucky or if we got Luke-y…as in money talks, and Luke knew how much I wanted to see the black sand.

Our tour guide, Marcus, clearly loves everything about Hawaii. He's enthusiastic while he tells us all about the Road to Hana in our private Jeep tour as he takes the twists and turns toward the historic town of Hana. It's about five hours one-way, and we stop at different beaches along the way…including the Wai'anapanapa black sand beach.

It's not soft, fine sand like we're traditionally used to when we think of beaches, but these are small black pebbles and rocks formed from the volcanoes. Marcus treats us to the history of the area, we snap about a million pictures of each other, and then we head back toward the hotel—another five hours in the Jeep, so by the time we get back, it's a little after nine at night.

We're both exhausted from fresh air and sitting in the car all day, but as Luke showers before I fall asleep, I study the pictures I took of him. I mark a few as favorites and potential thirst traps on Instagram, but really what I'm doing is looking at his smile.

In the first few from this morning, it starts out small.

By the time we got to the black sand, it was wider.

And by the time we hit our last stop as the sun started to set, it was a genuine, happy smile.

He's loosening up as we find a rhythm with each other. We spent the entire day together enjoying the scenery, laughing at the crazy things that came out of Marcus's mouth, and bonding. I'm not quite sure yet if we were bonding as friends or as a couple, but it certainly felt like the latter.

There were times today I thought he was going to kiss me, and then he backed away. There were times I had an urge to grab his hand, but I didn't. We keep getting so close to this imaginary line, and then we both seem to back away. I'm not sure why *he* backs away, but I know why I do.

I'm afraid he'll only reject me like he's already done before. A girl can only try so many times before she gets the hint and stops, and I'm almost to that point.

I may be falling for him, but he keeps sending signals that I'm the only one. And so, before I fall down a path from which I'll never be able to get up, before I get in too deep with him emotionally…I need to stop. I need to back slowly away or I'm going to get burned. In fact, the heat is already starting to smolder. It won't be long before that heat turns into a flame that has the power to scorch me.

* * *

Two days in the sun have wiped the two of us out. We're both exhausted at the dinner table as we dine at the same restaurant where our rehearsal dinner will be held in a couple nights.

The days may have been exhausting, but they were also fun. Thrilling. Adventurous. Filled with things of beauty—and I'm not just talking about the landscape, though that certainly gave my eyes many treats. We shared little moments that only served to bond the two of us. We built memories, things we can take with us even when this is all over. And that thought has me feeling a little melancholy tonight.

I put on the mask, though. I keep up the ruse like this is a good idea. But the more time I spend with Luke, the more I can see *this* as our future. I see Jeep tours and ATVs in Maui, or mountain climbing or skiing or relaxing in whatever other locations we visit.

I see hot days and sweaty nights, adventurous excursions followed by fists clenching sheets and fingerprints on windows.

"So ATV or zipline?" he asks, interrupting my internal musings. "Which did you like better?"

"I'm never going ziplining again," I mutter. "I still can't believe you talked me into doing it." He was very convincing. The fact that he took off his shirt might have had a little something to do with it, too. Hell, I might even do something crazier like bungee jumping from a bridge or skydiving out of a plane when he isn't wearing a shirt. My brain short-circuits and I can't make rational decisions when my eyes fall onto those abs.

He laughs. "And I even took pictures for evidence." He pulls out his phone. "Look at your face in this one. Priceless."

I look at myself and the sheer look of horror in my eyes and my mouth in a wide O shape as I started my ride across the beautiful plantation. Honestly it was prettier from the platform. I couldn't see it while I rode the line because my eyes were squeezed shut for the entire duration of the terrifying ride immediately after he took this picture.

"I'm posting the one of you throwing the devil horns with your fingers while your tongue is hanging out," I say. His abs are on-freaking-point in that one. Talk about a damn thirst trap.

He laughs. "Do what you need to."

I raise a brow. "Hawaii seems to be loosening you up. A few weeks ago, you never would've let me post that one."

"It's the rum," he says, nodding to the drink special of the night, a traditional Hawaiian mai tai.

I giggle. "I better post it before you change your mind," I say, taking out my phone. He stops me with a hand covering mine, and I can't help but feel the same pull of electricity I always feel when his hand is on mine.

"Before you post, just remember that as soon as you do, the seven hundred thousand people who've already found my account will all know we're in Hawaii," he says.

Damn. Being the publicist…that's definitely something I should've thought of. "I will also blame the mai tais on that one."

He laughs. "Let's take whatever pictures we want and save the posting for when we're back home."

I narrow my eyes at him. "Good call. Especially since your whole family will be here. Between you and your quarterback brother, there'd be a flood of sold-out flights heading toward Maui."

"Don't forget my dad. He coached college for years."

"Where'd he coach?" I ask. I take another sip of my drink. This is my second, and I'm already feeling the buzzing effects.

"Michigan. And Jack played for USC."

"So Wisconsin, Michigan, and USC? I don't know anything about college football but it sounds like big school rivalries."

He lifts a shoulder. "None are each other's biggest rival, but I played Jack when I was in college. I played my dad, too."

"Was that weird?"

He stares at his drink before he glances up to meet my eyes. "Not weird, exactly. But both Jack and I know a lot about my dad's coaching style, just like he knows a lot about our playing styles, so in some ways there were advantages and in other ways there were disadvantages. You always study your opponent, though, no matter who it is."

Our dinners are served, and a little food helps the buzzing in my head start to dissipate.

"What time do they get in tomorrow?" I ask.

"They're all getting in at different times. Kaylee made reservations tomorrow night so we'll just meet for dinner once everyone's here," he says. "I don't want to tell them about the wedding until the night before. That way no one has time to fuck it up."

I'm from the kind of family where I'd be waiting in the lobby with hugs for everyone's arrival. Clearly Luke is not from the same type of family, and not for the first time I can't help but wonder what, exactly, I'm marrying into.

Does it matter when it's all for show? I guess time will tell.

CHAPTER 13

I check myself in the mirror one last time. My skin glows from a few days in the sun, and the yellow dress I chose for tonight just enhances that glow. I draw in a deep breath. I'm nervous. I want them to like me even though it doesn't matter. I'm a people pleaser by nature, though, the kind of person who wants *everybody* to like her. And from the few snippets I've gotten about Luke's family, I'm not feeling too confident that they'll even care about me. Except maybe Kaylee.

I emerge from the bathroom and find Luke sitting on the chair in the corner, eyes trained on ESPN as usual. He wears jeans and a button-down shirt and even though he's totally casual, he looks dressy and delicious. My mouth waters as I drink him in before his eyes flick to me. And when they do...well, it seems like ESPN just doesn't matter anymore.

Something about the way he looks at me causes my knees to knock together. The heat in his gaze makes my stomach twist with even more nerves. It makes me wish this was all real...that he was feeling the same things I am.

He clicks off the television and stands. "Wow, Ellie," he says, his eyes sweeping down my form.

"Is that a good *wow*?" I ask, clearly fishing for a compliment.

"It's an incredible wow." He takes another step toward me, and then it's like he realizes what he's doing and stops short. He blows out a breath and finally glances away from me and toward the clock. "Should we head down?"

I nod as I try to push away the disappointment. "You ready for all this?" I ask.

He chuckles. "Nope. Not even a little."

"At least I won't be alone, then."

His mouth lifts in a small smile. "You're not alone."

I twist my lips and bite the inside of my cheek to keep the tears that seem to spring to my eyes at bay. That's the problem, isn't it? I'm very much alone in all this, and the thought is rather devastating.

We head toward the elevator, take it down to the lobby, and just before the doors open, he grabs my hand in his. My heart immediately lifts until my brain catches up. It's for show. This is what we'll do now. We'll play the parts. We'll put on the act. Meanwhile, my heart will take its beating and hopefully I'll be able to recover it by the time this whole thing is over.

Why am I doing this to myself?

I didn't allow that question to form in my mind until today. This moment. Right now.

Why am I putting myself through all this?

What am I getting out of it?

At first, it sounded fun. Marry the hot football guy, my older brother's best friend. That was back when this was all some big crush. But that big crush has become actual feelings, and he's been pretty clear that even though there's definitely something there between us, he's not going to act on it. This is nothing more than a business arrangement to him. To me, though, it's more than that.

I clutch his hand in mine as we walk toward the restaurant, and he mutters something under his breath as we get closer.

"What?" I ask.

"Jack's not here yet," he says through gritted teeth, and when I glance up at him, a smile is plastered across his lips. I may not know him *that* well, but I can tell the difference between real and fake. This one's fake. I force one of my own as we approach a party of three.

"Lu-Lu!" a gorgeous girl says. Long, dark hair cascades in pretty waves down to the middle of her back, and her blue eyes glow as they edge quickly to me. I see an immediate family resemblance between her and Luke.

His hand doesn't leave mine as his fake smile turns a bit more genuine. "Hey, Kay-Kay," he says, wrapping an arm around her shoulders as she tosses her arms around his neck. When he pulls back from their hug, he nods toward me. "I want to introduce you to someone," he says to his sister. "This is my fiancée, Ellie." He turns to me. "Ellie, Kaylee."

"So nice to meet you," I say, letting go of Luke's hand as I reach over for a hug.

"You too," she says. "I can't wait to get to know my future sister-in-law."

"This is the fiancée?" another female voice asks, and as I pull out of my hug with Kaylee, I'm faced with an older version of Kaylee except with a short, bob haircut and a few lines around her eyes. I smile as my eyes flick to the man who is obviously his dad. The resemblance is strong.

"Mom, Dad, this is Ellie," Luke says. He doesn't greet either of them with a hug, which surprises me.

"Carol Dalton," the older version of Kaylee greets me with her hand extended out to shake. I take hers in mine, and hers is cold.

"Nice to meet you," I say.

"Tim," his dad says, and we shake hands, too, which is followed by an awkward beat.

"So this is the girl you're marrying even though you got another girl pregnant?" Carol asks, her eyes appraising me shrewdly.

I choke on something at her question, and I glance over at my fiancé, who looks livid. "Mother," he says sharply, his voice a clear warning.

She raises a brow and purses her lips, but she doesn't say anything.

She doesn't apologize, but her son does. "I'm sorry, Ellie. That was out of line."

I shake my head, and I'm about to say it's fine when Tim pipes up. "Jack's on his way down now. We can go ahead and get our table."

Kaylee greets the hostess and we all follow along to a table in a private room, which is nice since I'm breaking bread with three celebrities, a younger sister, and my future mother-in-law. Luke clutches my hand as we walk, and when I glance over at him, his eyes are turned down to the ground. I can't tell if he's clutching my hand for show or if it has something to do with the fact that he just needs someone right now. And I'm someone. Enter Ellie or whatever.

I squeeze his hand, and he glances over at me. I see the gloom there in his eyes, one of the first times I can really read him well, and my heart aches for him. Seeing family should bring joy…not whatever this is. I give him a smile, and I squeeze his hand again just to let him know I'm right here for whatever he needs. We'll get through this together.

As far as first impressions go, Kaylee seems sweet, I haven't made up my mind on the dad, and the mom is basically terrible. I can't wait to find out where Jack falls in line with the rest of them.

Carol sits first. It's a rectangular table, and she chooses the chair at the head of the table. Tim settles at the other head of the table. Is that the tail?

Luke and I are facing the door, and he keeps glancing toward it as we all wait for his brother. I'm glancing through the menu when I hear a sharp intake of breath beside me as Luke seems to stiffen.

I look up at the doorway, and I draw in my own sharp intake of breath.

Sure enough, another member of this incredibly attractive family stands in the doorway. Intense navy eyes seem to hold a thunderstorm of emotions behind them, dark hair styled precisely, a strong jaw that's currently clenched with just enough groomed scruff to give him a bit of a mysterious edge, the same full lips his brother has.

Jack Dalton holds an air about him that commands attention, and he certainly has mine…as well as everyone else's at the table. He surveys his family, his eyes just sweeping past me like I'm of no importance to him, and he strides with self-assurance into the room. "Hello, Daltons," he says, his voice similar to Luke's deep and rich tone.

Tim stands to shake his son's hand, and my eyes fall to their connection. His hands are big like Luke's, and his fingers are long. I wonder how many footballs he's thrown in his life. I wonder how many women he's pleased with those hands. I shake that thought away as Tim claps Jack on the back. Carol stands, too, and she gives Jack a hug. Kaylee and Luke don't get up and it's just such a weird dynamic to me. Jack takes his seat.

"This is Ellie," Luke says. "My fiancée."

"I saw the headlines," Jack says shortly rather than something like *nice to meet you* or *welcome to the family.*

He doesn't introduce himself. Instead, he moves toward his seat like I'm just supposed to know who the hell he is. Well, newsflash asshole, I wouldn't have known a couple weeks ago.

"So, Luke, how'd you two meet?" Kaylee asks, clearly trying desperately to make things normal.

"She's Josh Nolan's sister." He says my brother's name like everyone at the table would know who that is, and they all do. I feel heat creeping into my cheeks as everyone's eyes turn to me. "And get this. She doesn't even watch football."

I glance around the table at the mix of surprised and horrified eyes as well as a couple of dropped jaws at that statement. I offer a smile with a little shrug. "I'm a unicorn."

Luke laughs and tosses an arm around the back of my chair, squeezing my shoulder. He leans over and presses a loving kiss to my temple, and my entire body warms. I glance at Jack, and I'm not sure why. He's watching the entire exchange. "You're more than a unicorn, babe."

"You guys are so cute," Kaylee says, obviously sealing in my instant love for her with that pronouncement.

I offer a nervous giggle, and before I can come up with some witty reply (which clearly isn't going to happen with the sheer number of intimidating people at this table), Jack speaks up. "Probably a smart move, Luke. The last two fanatics really fucked you over."

Luke pins him with a glare, but Jack just laughs.

We're saved when someone comes to take our dinner orders. I notice that Jack and Luke order the same thing—a medium steak with baked potato and broccoli. Must be some kind of football diet even in the offseason.

"What have you been up to this offseason, Jack?" Carol asks.

"We know what Luke's been up to," he says, raising his brows in my direction. When his eyes land on me, I feel...exposed. Branded. Nervous.

My cheeks redden further at his insinuation even though it's not true. Well, except for that one night.

"Stop," Luke says.

Long GAME

"I've been running drills with the new guys," he says, turning toward his mother to answer the question she posed. "Getting to know them and using my position as team captain to instill a sense of pride in our team." He glances at his brother. "But I don't want to give away too many secrets to the enemy."

Luke rolls his eyes. "What you do in the offseason isn't giving away any secrets."

"We understand, Jack," Tim says as if Luke never spoke at all. "We're just so proud of your accomplishments. Do you think the Broncos have a shot to win the big game again?" The way he says it clearly indicates that there's only one son at this table he's proud of, and my heart aches for Luke again.

He has his own accomplishments. He's a successful wide receiver. He plays pro football. He's a genuinely good guy. He's doing so much for me—giving me a place to live, giving me a job...giving me eye candy and thirst traps and spank bank material.

God, who knew that just being a witness to this family dinner could make me fall even more for the guy? I want to grab him into a hug and hold his hand and tell him that someone here cares about him. Someone here is proud of him. Someone here thinks the world of him.

That someone is me.

"More than a shot," Jack says to his father. "We traded for one of the top receivers in the league," he says, his eyes flicking to his brother as if to insinuate that Luke *isn't* one of the top receivers, "and combined with the speed of our draft picks and the skillset of our current team, we'll make an even stronger return. Expect a repeat."

Luke chuckles and shakes his head.

"What?" Jack asks, his tone a bit accusatory for someone who brims with such confidence.

"The Aces are in top shape, man. You'll have a fight on your hands for a repeat."

"Guess we'll find out which team is better twice next season," Jack says with a smirk. This time, it's not confidence as much as it's cockiness. Yet despite that, there's something incredibly charming about the guy. He's being a dick to his only brother, yet he does it with a smile that seems so damn genuine you can't help but think that somehow he's paying Luke a compliment even though he isn't.

My first impression of him is that he's someone who makes everyone in the room feel special just because they get to be in the same room as him. And somehow that includes me, even though he's barely glanced in my direction since he walked in except to make some sort of sexual insinuation about his brother.

I hate that it includes me. I don't want to like him because of how he treats his brother...yet I find myself incredibly fascinated by him. Incredibly attracted to him. Like I *want* him to look at me, to notice me.

His brother sure hasn't.

Jack dominates dinner conversation with tales of his big win and the celebrating that followed while Luke remains quiet. I learn that the Aces lost to Jack's team in the playoffs last year—the game that sent the Broncos to the Super Bowl. I learn that Jack likes women and he doesn't filter his words in front of his parents. I get the sense that Jack flirts with everyone—including our waitress, including a woman who walks by our doorway and recognizes him, including me when his eyes flick to mine from across the table as I sit next to his brother who I'm engaged to marry.

I learn that Luke is reserved in front of his family. He's not like that with me, though, which just tells me he's actually opened up to me even though he seems like such a closed book. I get it now, though—the reason *why* he's closed off. In his own family, he comes in second or third. Never first.

I just haven't figured out *why* that is yet.

CHAPTER 14

After what feels like an insufferable two hours, dinner is finally over. Jack leaves first, and I have no doubt it's because he has some woman chained to his bed that he needs to get back to. Just watching him cut his steak showed me how controlled and disciplined he is. He seems like the kind of guy who might have a secret kink if you know what I mean.

Tim orders one more cup of coffee even though the meal is over, and I glance at Luke as I'm unsure whether or not we have to stick around for more of this rare form of torture.

"Kaylee, would you mind hanging with Ellie by the lobby bar so I can talk to Mom and Dad alone for a few minutes?" Luke asks.

"I'd love to," Kaylee says, and she stands.

Luke leans over and presses a kiss to my cheek. "I'll be right there."

"Thanks so much for dinner," I say again to Tim, and he gives a short nod.

Kaylee links her arm through mine and we walk toward the bar, thankfully far away from Carol and Tim. "Congratulations on surviving your first dinner with them," she says, elbowing me a little in the ribs, and I giggle.

"Is it always that awkward?"

"Only when Jack and Luke are in the same room together," she says. "I'm sure he filled you in on their history."

"Not really," I admit. We slide onto the stools at the bar, which is fairly empty. "Just little tidbits here and there."

Her brows dip, and I guess as his fiancée, I should be more privy to all the inner workings of his family dynamic.

We each order a mai tai—probably a terrible idea since alcohol makes loose lips and I can't afford to admit the truth to Luke's sister for his sake, but after our first drink, the advantage is that *her* lips loosen, too. I sort of wonder how long Luke will be, but then Kaylee starts spilling all the tea once our second round arrives.

"Luke is my favorite brother, you know. I probably shouldn't pick, but Jack is just...he's Jack. He's my parents' favorite because he's the oldest, I'm the second favorite because I'm the youngest and the only girl, and Luke sort of just falls in the middle. He's such a good guy, so talented in football. But he tends to keep to himself. We could be such a close family. We try. Really, we do. I do, anyway. These annual vacations were my idea. It was the only way I got to see my very busy brothers when I was a pre-teen and they were just getting their starts in the league. And that's still true today. Do you know I haven't seen Luke since we were in New Zealand and I've only seen Jack once since then?"

I'm not sure whether that's rhetorical, and I don't want her to stop, so I just raise my brows and take a sip of my mai tai.

"We used to be closer before the whole Savannah thing went down between those two, and that's when their rivalry really started," she says.

"You mean the articles Savannah wrote?" I ask, proving I know at least a little something about the man I'm going to marry.

"The articles, yes, but all the other stuff, too," she says, lowering her voice. "It forced my parents to choose sides, and Luke came out the loser in all that. It pushed a divide between all of us. He stopped sharing the little parts of himself that he used to with us, it gave him trust and jealousy issues, and it wrecked his confidence."

My brows dip. What other stuff? What made him stop being himself around his own family? The articles probably gave him trust and jealousy issues, but what wrecked his confidence?

Being born into a family with someone like Jack probably set him up for low self-esteem. His own father favors his brother, and clearly his mom does, too. Were they like that his whole life?

Who builds him up when his family tears him down? The awful women he's been with before?

Enter Ellie.

I don't want to admit what I don't know, so I tuck it to the back of my mind for later. But I *will* be asking Luke about it.

She blows out a breath. "Anyway. Tell me about you. I've always wanted a sister and God knows Savannah and Michelle never fit that description."

I laugh. "What do you want to know?"

"Do you work?" she asks.

I nod. "I'm in PR and actually I'm handling your brother's publicity now."

"I saw his Instagram. It's freaking lit, Ellie. Is that all you?"

I nod and give a modest shrug. "Yeah. He didn't want one, but I talked him into it." I refrain from mentioning that he actually *needed* one to hit his goals. I'm not sure how much Luke would want me to share with his sister regarding all that—especially not if it gets back to his mom, and then his dad, and then back to Jack. He's right about the family politics. There's all sorts of shit I wasn't expecting up in here.

"God, if you could get him to do that..." she trails off, but her insinuation is that I'm a good match for him. It feels good that the one family member whose opinion he might actually respect thinks that of us. "When are you getting married?" she asks.

I freeze. It's our news to share together, but this is still his turf. He wanted to wait and tell everyone the night before, and it's up to me to respect that. Another mai tai might not have stopped me, though. "Oh, I don't know. You know Luke." I twist my lips and roll my eyes.

"What's that eyeroll supposed to mean?" the man himself asks. He must've snuck up behind me.

I jump, startled by his voice. "I didn't know you were standing there. Your sister was just asking me when the wedding is."

"Ah," he says, and then he shrugs. "We'll figure something out."

Good dodge, Luke.

"So why do you call him Lu-Lu?" I ask Kaylee.

She giggles. "I couldn't say *Luke* when I was little, so that's what I called him. It just stuck even though he frickin' *hated* it."

"Imagine this," he says, making a motion with his hands in the air. "A twelve-year-old boy with all his buddies over, and his two-year-old sister walks by yelling Lu-Lu! Lu-Lu!" He shakes his head with a chuckle.

Kaylee and I both giggle.

"What did you talk to Mom and Dad about?" Kaylee asks.

He rolls his eyes. "I told them to lay off Ellie. It's not her fault Michelle's knocked up."

"But it *is* yours," another voice similar to Luke's says.

Luke grits his teeth then clenches his jaw as we all turn to see Jack standing behind us. He flicks a finger in the air to the bartender, who dashes over to tend to the man who owns the entire room just because he's in it. It's truly some phenomenon to witness.

He orders a gin and tonic. I've never seen anyone order anything with gin in it before, and somehow it brings another level of sophistication. Luke orders a beer when the bartender's eyes flick to him.

If we were at this same bar without Jack, I can't help but think that Luke would be the man owning the room. He's more laid back than his brother, and definitely not as arrogant, but the brothers do share some of the same qualities. Ridiculous good looks, athletic ability, and those navy blue eyes, for starters, plus this intrinsic charisma—though the brothers express that charisma in totally different ways.

I feel suddenly nervous that he's here. He somehow throws everything into a tailspin with just his presence…even though I have to admit that I'm curious what this dynamic will look like without the parents around.

"Nice of you to join us," Luke says.

Jack slides onto the open stool next to Kaylee. "Figured I could spare some time for a drink with my favorite siblings." His eyes fall onto me, and my chest races. "Plus the future Mrs. Dalton."

Heat creeps up my spine, and I take a sip of my mai tai to try to cool down.

"When's the wedding?" Jack asks.

I glance at Luke desperately for the answer. He gives a similar vague reply. "We're working on it."

Jack barks out a laugh. "That's noncommittal. I thought you weren't getting married again."

It's not a question, but Luke treats it like one. "I wasn't. And then I met Ellie." His arm is around the back of my chair, and it slides to my shoulder. He draws me into a side hug, and it all feels a little territorial—as it should since we're putting on the show now even for his family.

"Seems fast," Jack comments, and the bartender returns with the drinks.

"It is," I admit. "But when you know..."

"You know," Luke finishes, and he pins me with a loving gaze that makes me momentarily forget that Kaylee and Jack are right beside us.

Jeez. If this is an act, Luke deserves the Oscar.

"Finishing each other's sentences already. Precious." Jack's final word drips with sarcasm, and Luke leans over to press a kiss to my temple.

"Jealousy is ugly on you," Luke says.

Jack scoffs with a grunt, but he doesn't respond to Luke's claim, and suddenly I feel like a bit of a pawn in Luke's little game with his brother.

Was that always part of the motivation here? To marry me in front of his family, but more specifically, in front of Jack?

Why would that make Jack jealous? He could have anyone he wanted.

Although Kaylee mentioned something about there being more with Savannah...did Jack want Luke's wife?

Questions swirl around my head, but I have zero answers and a pretty strong buzz from the mai tai.

Luke stands suddenly and grabs my hand. "We're going to head out."

"We're just getting started," Jack says, draining his entire gin and tonic in practically one sip.

"Maybe you are," Luke says, "but my fiancée and I are going to call it a night, if you know what I mean."

Jack raises a brow in a way that totally makes it clear he got Luke's underlying meaning.

"You two are adorable," Kaylee says. "Have fun, kids."

Long GAME

"And be safe," Jack says, eyes forward as he motions to the bartender for a refill. "This family doesn't need another baby scandal."

"Fuck you, Jack," Luke says quietly—venomously—and then he yanks my hand into his and leads me away from the bar.

CHAPTER 15

Instead of leading me up to our hotel room, Luke stalks toward the doors that exit to the pool. Clearly he's upset after his brother's words. I see it in the way his shoulders are hunched, in the way he's walking too fast for me to really keep up especially after a few mai tais while I'm wearing heels, and in the pinch of his brows.

He walks past the pool, and finally I yell at him, "Slow down!"

He stops, and I run into him a little. "Sorry," he mutters, and then he keeps walking. When we get to the beach, he slips off his shoes and socks, and I take off my heels. We leave them in the sand, and he grabs my hand again.

He draws in a deep breath, and he blows it out slowly as we stroll slowly toward the water. The beach is deserted at this late hour, but it's lit by the lights coming from the hotel just behind us. His hand isn't in mine anymore, but then there's not really anybody out here for us to continue putting on the show for.

"What the hell am I marrying into?" I finally ask.

He grunts out a chuckle even though it's not very funny, but that's his only response.

"You want to tell me about what's going on between the two of you?" I ask once our toes touch the water.

He clears his throat as he stares down at the gentle waves rolling over his toes. "Not really."

"Kaylee said Savannah came between you and Jack," I try again, "and she made it sound like there was more to it than you told me." I leave that out there for him to expand upon, and he just quietly stares into the water. I let him gather his thoughts, and then because I can't take the silence, I say, "Talk to me, Luke."

He sighs. "I've lived in Jack's shadow my entire life. When Jack wouldn't commit to Savannah, she turned to me to make him jealous. I was young, stupid, and horny. I thought she wanted me for me. Turns out she only wanted my brother."

My head whips in his direction. "What?"

He nods and presses his lips together. "She was with him first. They were together almost a year when he dumped her, and she came to me as a shoulder to cry on. I fell for her. I chose her over my family. That's when my parents chose Jack. They thought I was the dick who stole Savannah away when the truth was that she was a conniving bitch who said all the right things to make me think it was me she wanted all along. That was far from the truth, and now I'm stuck paying alimony to a woman who only ever loved my brother and the spotlight."

"Oh my God," I murmur, shocked by this new revelation.

"See?" he says, and he pats his chest. "I'm no prince."

"She tricked you, Luke," I say. "That doesn't pull you from the prince category."

"As I've been reminded constantly, I chose her over my family. I broke family code when I slept with my brother's ex even though he told me at the time he was okay with it. I felt like shit after the first time I slept with her, but I called Jack the next morning. I was honest with him from the start. He told me he was fine with it, and eventually he agreed to being spotlighted in her articles."

"Why would he do that?" I ask. The waves wash over my feet, burying them in wet sand, and I pull them up out of the sand so the process can start over.

"I don't know. Maybe because he still cared about Savannah. They were together a long time, and he wanted her to have a successful career. We both knew the reach a story about the two of us could have since we were brothers in the league together with a fairly well-known father. Or maybe because he knew I'd come out looking like the asshole and he loved any chance he had to take the spotlight."

"So were you private even before she printed all that stuff about you two?"

He lifts a shoulder. "I guess I've always been that way. We're a famous family, but we're not perfect. We all have secrets we'd prefer to keep hidden."

"What are yours?" I ask softly.

"Aside from marrying Savannah?" He grunts. "Stories for another day."

So there *are* more secrets in his closet. Interesting.

I'm not sure what to do with the revelations from tonight, though.

"What are Jack's?" I ask.

He kicks at the sand. "Not my secrets to tell."

We're quiet a beat, and then because I'm me and my filter often malfunctions particularly after alcohol, I ask the question that first came to mind at the bar. "So this wedding, and me...is this all just a game to one up your brother?"

He clears his throat, and then he blows out a breath. "I wouldn't call it a *game*," he says. "But it *is* an opportunity. We were going to do this anyway, and the timing just worked out. I get to flaunt my happy ending with my beautiful bride in front of my entire family. A bride who, by the way, has no prior affiliation with my brother. She's all mine. It's a fresh start.

Besides, what's more romantic than a wedding on the beach in Maui?"

"Even if you don't have real feelings for that bride?" I press.

"They don't have to know that." He shrugs with nonchalance, and it only serves to piss me off.

I nod and press my lips together as I try to process all that. It shouldn't hurt...but it does. I should be thankful for his honesty...but I'm not.

Instead, I'm left wondering whether I should really be doing this. All the breakthroughs over the last couple days, the bonding, the fun...it feels like it was all just part of his plan.

Luke doesn't love me. He doesn't want me. He doesn't have feelings for me, as he just made abundantly clear.

I'm not even totally sure he even *cares* about me.

But how do I back out at this point? He may not have feelings for me, but it's not like I can just shut off mine for him. And even if I could, then what? Move back to Chicago?

It's not like I have a home or a job that doesn't intertwine with Luke Dalton in Vegas. I could stay there, but I'm risking my career all over again after everything that happened in Chicago not so long ago. I finally have a *celebrity* client. This could open up so many doors for me, and all I have to do is just go through with what we already have planned.

But his admission hurts. His words cut. Maybe they shouldn't, but my feelings are involved even if his aren't.

"Glad the timing worked out for your opportunity," I say, and then I spin on my heel, run up the beach, grab my shoes, and head in the direction of the hotel room I'm sharing with him.

I'll call Nicki. She's on her honeymoon, but I need to talk to someone about this. I'm desperate, and if this isn't an emergency, I don't know what is. What the hell am I supposed to do?

I brush away a tear as I pass by the pool.

Should I go through with this ridiculous plan?

I already know what Nicki will say. The obvious answer is *no*. I'm only hurting myself.

I refuse to let more tears fall until I'm up in my room. I beeline for the elevator. I need to get the hell out of here before some other Dalton sees me crying in the lobby after Luke just admitted he doesn't have feelings for me.

But fate apparently has other plans.

Just as I hit the button to call the elevator, a voice sounds behind me. It sounds like Luke's, but it's not. It's deeper. More confident. "Going up to bed alone?"

I spin around, my feet still bare and my shoes in my hand. "That's not your business." My voice is a hiss, and I'm not sure why I'm so defensive when Jack has no idea what just went down between Luke and me. I haven't even had thirty seconds to myself to process whether I'm overreacting, so of course I had to run into him.

Jack smirks, and I wish his face wasn't so goddamn handsome. "You're marrying my brother. Sounds like it *is* my business."

"I'm not Savannah," I spit at him.

"Or Michelle." He laughs, but I don't get the joke.

Or Michelle?

What the hell is that supposed to mean?

Did *Jack* sleep with Michelle?

Is Michelle really pregnant with Luke's baby?

Or is it...Jack's?

Before I can ask that question, he leans in a little closer and lowers his voice. "So he filled you in on our history, did he?" He's close enough that I can smell him, some woodsy and masculine scent mixed with hot danger and gin. He lowers his voice. "Did he tell you *everything*?"

"Of course he did," I lie, and I'm not even sure why I'm lying after what he just said to me out on that beach. I'm angry with him. I'm hurt and I'm sad. Yet here I am, protecting him and our lie as Jack puts me on the spot—a place where I'm incredibly uncomfortable because honestly I don't know Luke well enough to defend him. He hasn't let me get to know him—not the *real* him, anyway.

The elevator doors open, but I don't step on. I'm rooted to the spot as Jack penetrates me with his gaze.

He raises a brow as his mouth curls into a lazy smile, and it's sly and salacious and definitely flirtatious. "Good. Then you know how we like to share. I'm in room twenty-six-oh-nine if you're up for some fun. I can promise you a hell of a good time...better than whatever my little brother gives you."

He gets onto the elevator, and his raised brow is a clear invitation that I should go up to his room with him.

Luke doesn't want me.

But Jack seems to.

I don't want to be part of this game between the two of them, but suddenly I'm sucked into this world I didn't even know existed a few minutes ago. Suddenly I have two brothers pulling at me from different sides, neither of them pretending like this is something more than it is.

I don't know whether I want either of them while I'm sure I want them both. How lucky is Savannah that she got to experience a life with both men? Not just for their talents or how fucking hot they are or their fame or money...but because she got to know each man and who he is on the inside, she got both to fall in love with her, and she got to share a bed with both of them.

And Michelle, too?

That could be me next…except *neither* man wants me for me. They want me for how they could use me to one-up their brother.

I shouldn't get on with him. I shouldn't share that small space with Jack Dalton, not with the tempting invitation he just issued when I'm *engaged* to his brother.

I don't know if I can continue this lie with Luke.

Despite how hurt I feel right now, I still want to protect him from his family. I still want to help him with this Michelle mess.

But I'm not entirely sure I can marry him.

To be continued in book 3, **FAIR GAME.**

ACKNOWLEDGMENTS

Thank you to my husband for everything you do. The support, encouragement, and love is what makes this possible. Thank you to my kids for nap time and quiet time when mommy gets to write, and thank you to my parents who love hanging out with my babies so I can get some computer time in.

Thank you to Trenda London from It's Your Story Content Editing, Diane Holtry and Alissa Riker for beta reading, Najla Qamber for the gorgeous cover design, and Katie Harder-Schauer from Proofreading by Katie.

Thank you to Wildfire Marketing, my ARC team, Team LS, and all the bloggers who read, post, and review.

Thank you to you, the reader, for taking time out of your life to spend it with Ellie. I hope you enjoyed what you read, and I can't wait for you to read the next book.

xoxo,
Lisa Suzanne

ABOUT THE AUTHOR

Lisa Suzanne is a romance author who resides in Arizona with her husband and two kids. She's a former high school English teacher and college composition instructor. When she's not cuddling or chasing her kids, she can be found working on her latest book or watching reruns of *Friends*.

ALSO BY LISA SUZANNE

A LITTLE LIKE DESTINY
A Little Like Destiny Book One
#1 Bestselling Rock Star Romance

TAKE MY HEART
My Favorite Band Book One
#1 Bestselling Rock Star Romance

Printed in Great Britain
by Amazon